Praise for *Every Ver*

"Chaudhry has a knack for capt
towns and how gossip turns into
goes in a really satisfying directio............................ ....

 **Fiona Barnett, author of** *The Dark Between the Trees*

"*Every Version Ends in Death* is a hauntingly beautiful ghost story that explores life, death, and, most importantly, the in-between. As Aliya Chaudhry delves deep into the mystery at the crux of her novel, the lines between the living and the dead blur, revealing a poignant reflection on female grief, memory, and the stories we leave behind. This is a Gothic feminist power-house of a novel that will leave you spellbound, challenging your notions of hauntings and humanity along with the women who shape our world."

 **Lauren T. Davila, author & anthology editor**

"In this thoughtful meditation on death, Aliya Chaudhry finds beauty in both the mundane and the morbid."

 **Diversity in Horror**

"A thoughtful meditation on the things, people and events that haunt us. Chaudhry gently leads us on a journalistic approach to ghost hunting – sifting through urban legends, historical documents and conversations with old friends – to uncover the truth."

 **Rhiannon Grist, author of** *The Queen of the High Fields*

"Quietly haunting. *Every Version Ends in Death* explores the challenges of adolescence and the realities of growing up through the lens of guilt, grief and obsession."

 **Joanna Corrance, author of**
The Gingerbread Men **and** *John's Eyes*

Published by Haunt Publishing
hauntpublishing.com
@HauntPublishing

ISBN (paperback): 978-1-915691-07-1
ISBN (ebook): 978-1-915691-08-8

Cover design by Caroline Devereaux:
catandmilk.com

Typeset by Laura Jones-Rivera:
lauraflojo.com

Printed and bound in Great Britain by Clays Ltd, Elcograf S.p.A.

Every Version
Ends in Death

Aliya Chaudhry

For my father, who loves history, and
for my mother, who played in graveyards.
I guess it's not really that weird I wrote this book.

Content note

death; grief; murder reference; loss of a loved one;
suicide reference

Chapter 1

It was hard to go home. It had nothing to do with the town – even though it was pretty small, far away, and thoroughly unexciting – or the people, or the fact that I hadn't been back in a while. It's just that it was my home, it was filled with my memories, and it knew everything about me. I had learned everything there. Everywhere I went, every corner I turned, I saw myself doing something there years ago – talking, running, riding a bike, falling off that bike, learning to drive.

Belonging is terrifying.

★ ★ ★

"Hey, what's with the sign?" I asked as we drove by the gates that had sealed shut what we all knew to be an enormous yet fantastically creepy house. I couldn't make out what it said. I couldn't see the house either, only the gate, looking skeletal now they had cleared all the ivy.

"It's haunted," Dad said.

"People have been saying that for years," I said. "They don't need a sign for that."

"I think they're tearing it down," Mom said.

"That's what they think," Dad said. "They won't succeed – why?"

"Because it's haunted," Mom said.

"What makes it so haunted?" I said.

"Everyone says so," Dad said.

"Just saying something's haunted doesn't make it haunted," I said.

"There's a ghost," Mom said.

"Yeah, sure there's a ghost," I said. "Again, isn't it just a story?"

"People love a good story," Dad said.

"And even more than that, they love making up stories," Mom said.

★ ★ ★

I'm not sure why I dreaded coming back to Clifton so much. Sairah and I always used to talk about leaving, couldn't wait to get out, but I never hated living here. I wasn't that sad to leave, either. Years later, I did, however, hate the thought of visiting. Probably because there were too many memories. Too many I-should-haves and what-ifs and oh-remember-thats. Too many reminders of who I used to be. Too many people who would look at me and see the me from ten, fifteen, twenty years ago. Weirdly, it felt like taking a step back, even though progress isn't measured in literal distance.

★ ★ ★

My mother had been the first person to tell me the story. Hayward Manor sat in between the children's hospital and the ice cream shop we would go to after all required immunisations. One day in kindergarten, when we were sitting on the side of the creek after a visit to the doctor, I asked my mother about the old house.

"The story is that there was a nurse who lived there. There weren't any hospitals back then so sometimes she used to take care of people in her house. She was really hard-working and liked helping people."

"What happened to her?" I asked, between licks of my ice-cream cone.

"Well, the problem is that when someone in the house is sick, the other people living with them might get sick too. And so, she got really sick, and because they didn't have the right medicines back then, she couldn't get better," Mom said.

"Oh, that's so sad."

"It is. She helped a lot of people, though. That's why the house is still there. To remember her."

"And now it's haunted? By her?"

"Some people think so. Some people think they've seen her."

I looked around at the landscape that gave Creek Hill its name. I couldn't see any signs of her. I hung my head. "How come I never get to see her?"

My mom laughed. "You want to see her? You're not scared?"

I shrugged. "She doesn't seem scary to me. You said she took care of people. She sounds nice."

★ ★ ★

When I heard a friend tell the story at a sleepover a year later, I corrected her.

"Her house caught on fire," Rhea said.

"No, that's not true," I said.

"Yes, it is," she said.

"Her house is still there," I said. "It's not burnt."

"How do you know? You can't see it."

"She was a nurse and got sick and died."

"No, I'm pretty sure there was a fire."

"Maybe she got sick and then there was a fire?"

★ ★ ★

A quick Google search pulled up this article:

Creek Hill House Set for Demolition
The historic house at the end of Creek Hill Road is set for demolition at the end of the month.

The house, also known as Hayward Manor, belonged

to the Hayward family, who were one of the first families to settle in the area and were among the founders of Clifton. In 1860, Charles and Annabelle Hayward founded the first hospital in Clifton, Hayward Hospital, now called Clifton Primary Care.

In 1879, a fire killed Charles, Annabelle and their twenty-nine-year-old daughter, Carolyn. Carolyn has become the inspiration for a famous ghost tale, making the house a local attraction.

The article was dated 2014. But there was a comment I recognised:

Jay Norcott: Don't worry, Carolyn will keep them out.

★ ★ ★

I messaged Jay. "How did that story go again?"

"She was a nurse."

"And?"

"Her patients all died, and she blamed herself for their deaths. The guilt and grief were overwhelming. She hung herself."

"You sure?"

"That's what Wikipedia says."

★ ★ ★

I went on Wikipedia. "The Ghost of Creek Hill" rerouted to Carolyn Hayward. It said:

In the spring of 1882, Carolyn accompanied her parents on a trip to Baltimore. They died as a result of an accident while travelling back.

I clicked the link on the superscript next to "back." An article from *The Chronicle* opened up. It was written twelve years ago.

> *The Haywards were some of Clifton's earliest residents.*
> *They were a wealthy family who, in 1849, built the first*
> *hospital in the town, Hayward Hospital, later renamed Clif-*
> *ton Hospital and now called Clifton Children's Hospital.*
>   *Carolyn Hayward, the daughter of the hospital's found-*
> *ers, Charles and Annabelle Hayward, was a nurse who*
> *worked in the hospital until her death in 1883, while trav-*
> *elling with her parents to Philadelphia.*

* * *

My mom lived near the cemetery when she first moved to Clifton for university. She told me stories about jumping over the fence and walking among the graves and weeds with her friends, all of them in a competition to spook the others. Jumping out and making phantom noises, pretending to be ghosts. They would scream and then laugh, scared by the living more than the dead.

I had broken into the cemetery as a teenager. I was staying at Amara's house, and we had heard one too many songs that talked about hanging out in graveyards. She lived a block away. We told her parents we were catching a late movie and walked there instead. At that point, the cemetery was open to the public during the day, but closed at night, which is when we preferred to visit. They had made the fence a little taller then, probably because of the aforementioned trespassers who now had trespassing kids of their own. I had to give Amara a boost over the high wrought-iron gates. Then I climbed up and clambered down the other side. We had flashlights, but there were lights in the cemetery. I remember thinking it would be full of fog, but it wasn't. It was dark, but clear. We found a patch of grass to sit on.

"We should have brought snacks," she said.

"Do you think we're being disrespectful?" I asked.

"We're just sitting," she whispered.

Even back then, I didn't believe in ghosts. I just remembered it being really quiet and weirdly unexceptional in any way. Just a dark patch of grass at night. It didn't feel eerie or haunted or sad or scary. We could be sitting in my garden, or on Amara's lawn, or even in her living room with the lights off in our sleeping bags, like we would later that night.

I went for jogs around the cemetery during my breaks from college. In junior year, my off-campus apartment had also been near a cemetery. These jogs always ended up being much longer runs because I would inevitably get lost and have to find my way out. Or I would underestimate how long it would take to get out, wouldn't budget enough time, didn't calculate when I was supposed to turn around. That cemetery was expansive, with winding paths and different-sized sections. There were no maps, and my GPS would always put me five yards away from where I really was. I'd just keep running until I found my way out.

But this cemetery was neater, more organised, more contained. I did laps around the area, not venturing in between the graves. It didn't feel any different than it had on any other jog, but I was trying hard not to get too close to any of the graves. My impulse to look won over my will to not see, and I caught a glance of the one part that had changed.

The flowers were still on Daadi's grave, only half-decayed from when my mother had placed them there three days before.

* * *

The plaque in front of Hayward Manor read:

> *Hayward Manor, also called the House on Creek Hill, was one of the first houses built in Clifton. The Hayward family resided here for three generations. In 1829, Charles and*

Annabelle Hayward founded the local hospital. They died ten years after it opened. They were survived by a daughter, Carolyn Hayward, who used to work in the hospital. Her story became a local legend. She was believed to have died in a fire at the hospital.

Note: This property is protected by the City of Clifton.

★ ★ ★

"Laana?"

I was browsing cereal boxes in the grocery store, trying to remember which ones my parents liked, and what the rest of them tasted like. I turned around quickly to face Faiz.

"You're still here?" He was still annoyingly tall. We were the same height and then suddenly I was taller, until he shot up at the end of middle school and I never caught back up.

"Yeah, I barely left. I mean, I moved back right after college. How have you been? How are your parents?"

"Good, except, you know."

"Right, I heard. I'm so sorry."

"Thanks."

"How does it feel to be back?"

"Like I never left."

"Really? I feel like nothing's stopped changing."

★ ★ ★

I looked up the house on the city's website of preserved landmarks when I got home.

Hayward Manor was one of the first houses built in Clifton. It belonged to the Hayward family, who settled in Connecticut in the 1790s. Charles and Annabelle Hayward opened the first hospital in the town, Hayward Hospital, now Clifton Hospital. They died in 1881 in a fire. Their daughter,

Carolyn, went on to work at the hospital and open the first children's wing there. She mysteriously passed away in 1883.

The death of Carolyn Hayward resulted in the entire Hayward savings being transferred to the hospital. Her death is a source of local legend, but there are competing theories. The actual cause of her death was unknown.

★ ★ ★

Sometimes it feels like people don't die at once, but erode little by little. Fragment, dissipate piece by piece. I know that, physically, they die suddenly. But they're not dead in the minds of others. It takes time for everyone to find out, to accept it.

And then, it doesn't feel like they're gone. They're not here, but maybe they were never here. Maybe they didn't live near you, you hadn't seen them in a while, you were never really close. It feels like maybe they just live far away, like they moved.

Sometimes it still feels like they're alive.

★ ★ ★

Sairah and I met at the coffee shop we used to do homework at in high school. It still had the same name, but the sign was different. They had repainted the walls, replacing the black paint with flowery white wallpaper. String lights had come up. The entire space had been rearranged. They had replaced the larger wooden tables with small circular ceramic ones.

Sairah was already sitting there when I walked in. She was writing furiously in a mint-green leather notebook, head bent over, dark hair tied back like it always was. She knew I'd be late. She knew that I hadn't gotten any better at showing up on time.

"Let me get your coffee – caramel latte?" she asked. I nodded with a slightly embarrassed smile. "Don't you love consistency?" she said as she walked towards the counter.

"Don't you mean, 'don't you hate change?'" I asked when she came back.

"Who doesn't?" she said, sitting down.

"Speaking of change," I said. "Everything here still feels the same. Does it feel that way to you?"

"Clifton has changed. But I feel like I haven't changed. I do all the things I used to do. I have the same hobbies. I sit in the same room I've always sat in doing what I always did. Everything around me is changing. I'm staying still."

"I wish things had stayed more still."

"I know."

★ ★ ★

Long after we had finished our cups of coffee, we found ourselves wandering through the park.

"It's so weird," I said. "I expected things to be different, feel different. But it's as if I'm still fifteen."

"Nothing ever changes in Clifton," Sairah said.

"That's not true," I said.

"This town is stuck. Nothing comes, nothing goes, we're all trapped."

"What about that apartment block?" I pointed across the street.

"It was built when we were in high school."

"The bookstore?"

"Celebrated its ten-year anniversary last May."

"Cineplex?"

"Renovated three years ago. But it has that sign saying it's been open since 2000."

"School?"

"Went back to talk to the kids about university and it felt like I hadn't even graduated high school yet. Even the lunch tables are in the same arrangement."

I tried to think of other examples. I opened my mouth and then closed it.

"We are stuck in some old town, frozen in time. Even our local ghost is over a hundred years old. We haven't had any new ghosts."

★ ★ ★

NOTICE: HAYWARD HOUSE SCHEDULED FOR DEMOLITION
The City Council of Clifton has set the demolition of Hayward House for the end of October 2015.

Below it, another sign said: *The demolition has been delayed until December 2015.*

A notice below it said: *The demolition is scheduled for June 2016.* The original month had been papered over by "June", which was now crossed out. Above it, someone had written "September". I guess they eventually stopped trying to update it.

★ ★ ★

I had begun seeing ghosts. Not in the sense that I saw my grandmother walking around the house. But I saw her in my face when I looked in the mirror. In my father's voice when he told us he'd see us later. In the curls on our heads. In my mother's turn of phrase when I knocked over a dish. In my father's expression when he struggled to open a jar of olives. I wondered if when other people saw us, they saw the dead as well. I wondered if we haunted them the way we haunted each other.

★ ★ ★

"Do you remember the story of Carolyn from that creepy house on Creek Hill?" I said to Amara on a FaceTime call from my childhood bedroom.

"Oh yeah, the Creep Hill Killer?" she said from her apartment in Chicago.

"What?" I responded. "She didn't kill people."

"She totally did."

"That's absurd."

"Of course she did. This is a ghost story."

"So, she killed people while she was alive? Or after she died?"

"The first. That's why she became a ghost. Too much guilt."

★ ★ ★

My parents had never moved. I had spent my whole life until the age of eighteen in that house. As I walked through, I could remember where I lost a tooth, where I fell down and twisted my ankle, where I was when I opened my college acceptance letter, my parents on either side of me. I remembered running scared through the dark hallway, avoiding the creaky step on the staircase, slamming the door of my bedroom shut, lugging my suitcase in from the city.

I didn't just remember it, I felt it again, like it was the first time, all at once. As if I was stuck. But also, as if I was all of these people, all of these things and feelings at once.

★ ★ ★

"What's the version you heard?" I asked.

"She jumped out of the window," Sairah said. "Suicide."

"What were the other versions?" I asked.

"I heard so many," Sairah said. "I think at some point I combined them in my head. Like, I remember something about a fire. But then that was when we were little and they were teaching us about fire safety."

"Yeah, I remember that."

"So, for a while I thought she jumped out of the window because there was a fire or something like that. But then I think maybe an adult told me that as a child so they wouldn't have to explain suicide to me." After a pause, Sairah continued. "I don't know what's real. I don't even know if she existed. People will construct almost anything."

★ ★ ★

I saw Carolyn every time I went for a run. She had a huge gravestone, one of those ornate, enormous marble sculptures. It was a giant statue of her or, I guess, what was supposed to be her. There was no way to confirm, but it didn't really match up to the few illustrations or photos I had seen of her. I wondered who made the decision to mark her grave with a statue. Her parents died before her. She didn't have any other family. She died alone. Or did she? Did she have friends who didn't make it into the ghost stories and history books?

Every time I saw her, I made a left. She was at the corner of a big hill of gravestones, standing out to denote her own importance.

★ ★ ★

"Okay, so I asked my mom," Sairah said, as we browsed the farmer's market.

"What did she say?" I asked, lifting up a jar of some kind of jam.

"She died of a broken heart."

"Sounds like something a man would come up with about a woman," I said, moving on to the next stall.

"Aren't you even a little bit curious who broke her heart?"

"Umm... maybe her parents dying?"

"Or?"

"Or what?"

"The kind of person most statistically likely to have killed a woman."

★ ★ ★

I walked into the hospital. The walls had been painted a friendly turquoise, rather than the clinical white and sombre beige of my childhood doctor appointments. Everyone was bustling around as usual. There was a mural where the community bulletin board used to be. Tigers and monkeys peered out from brightly coloured, well-defined, uniform leaves. Their eyes looked more googly than real, but they stared out from the acrylic layer and searched my soul. *Don't bother*, I felt like telling them, *there's not much here but guilt and grief.* Opposite the mural was a set of pamphlets. I grabbed one titled "The History of the Hospital".

There was a sepia photo of Hayward Manor on it. The photo's starkness made the house seem even more eerie. The background was that absent shade of beige, outdone in blandness by the Times New Roman font used. I opened it and started reading.

> *Clifton Children's Hospital was originally called Hayward Hospital and treated patients of all ages. It was named after its benefactors, Charles and Annabelle Hayward, whose daughter, Carolyn, worked in the hospital as a nurse and, later, in a management position.*
>
> *Hayward Hospital was renamed Clifton Hospital in the 1950s, as the town of Clifton grew, and the neighbouring towns opened their own hospitals. It was renamed Clifton Children's Hospital in 1981.*

On the opposite flap, there was a portrait of Carolyn, her hair in a tight bun, her features severe and her face expressionless, alongside a description of her:

> *The daughter of two of the hospital's founders, Carolyn always had an interest in nursing and caretaking. She graduated at the top of her class from the New England College*

of Nursing and came back home to work. She created the children's wing of the hospital. She worked at Hayward Hospital and lived in Clifton until her mysterious death in 1876.

★ ★ ★

I was at Sairah's house when her sister Hena called on FaceTime.

"You remember Creepy Carolyn?" Sairah shouted into the screen, her mouth full of cereal. Hena nodded and Sairah handed the phone to me.

"Do you remember how the story went?" I asked.

"Yeah, she drowned," Hena said.

"In the bath?" I asked.

"No, in the lake," Hena said.

"We don't have any lakes here, stupid," Sairah said.

"I meant the river," Hena said.

"It's a creek," Sairah corrected.

"The creek, then, whatever it is," Hena said.

"Was it suicide?" I asked.

"No," Hena said. "It was a witch trial."

"A witch trial?" Sairah and I said in unison, looking at each other.

"Yeah," Hena said. "If a woman was thought to be a witch, they would put her in water to test it out. If she didn't drown, she was a witch. But then if she did—"

"We know what the witch trials were, thank you very much," Sairah said.

"So, she drowned," I said. "She wasn't burned at the stake?"

"Drowning was what I heard," Hena said.

"That doesn't make any sense," Sairah said to me. "Is it even the right time period?"

"We're in the right place for it, geographically," I said to Sairah. I turned back towards the phone. "Hena, do you have any idea why she was accused of being a witch?"

Hena and Sairah both said in unison, "She was too smart."

"Come to think of it, it must have been really easy to accuse people of witchcraft. All you had to do was stand out a little bit, go against someone in some way. Not necessarily challenge them, but do something you weren't supposed to."

"And then everyone turns against you," Sairah said. "For something you didn't even do."

★ ★ ★

As I walked through the park on my way to the record store, I had flashes of memories. I saw myself attempting to learn volleyball with my dad, the ball careening into the bushes. I saw Amara on a bike, on the way to her house after school. I saw Faiz and Sairah fighting as we walked together. I remembered Devon trying to find shade to lie down in on a busy Saturday afternoon. I saw my mom pulling my wagon full of library books. One of the wheels was permanently squeaky; one corner looked like someone had crumpled it and smoothed it out, like aluminium foil, after I had dinged it against too many lamp posts and concrete walls.

Another memory came back to me:

"Carolyn Hayward was a witch!" Devon shouted with a smile. I laughed in response.

"Untrue," a fifteen-year-old Sairah countered.

"Can you prove it?"

"No, that's the whole problem. All of the witch tests ended in death."

"All I'm saying is we don't know what happened," Devon said. "She lived in a house by herself, alone."

"She definitely had patients she treated," Sairah said.

"She could have healed them with magic," Devon said. "Who says witches have to be evil?"

"Like, every story," I said.

"Were they witches or were they just women?" Sairah asked.

"Or were they just weird?" Devon laughed.

"It just sounds like an excuse," Sairah huffed. "For everyone to gang up against a woman."

"But Devon, do you know what actually happened to her?" I asked.

"She was just a regular nurse at the hospital. Then she went missing. Some people think she was kidnapped, others think she ran away."

"Why would someone want to kidnap a nurse?"

"She was rich. Ransom money."

"Didn't her parents die before her?" Sairah said.

Devon ignored her and went on with the story. "Nobody knew where she went. She got far away from Clifton, started a new life and died years and years later."

"Ugh, I wish I could do that," Sairah said. We looked at her. "Escape, I mean. I feel like I'm gonna be stuck here forever."

"Well, she's kinda stuck here now," Devon said. "She's been here for over a century."

* * *

I reached the record store ten minutes later, though I felt I had travelled back and forth ten years. I went over to the second-hand section, to see if there was anything that caught my interest.

"Look who finally returned," a voice behind me said.

I turned around, saw Taylor and smiled. She looked the same as she had when we were younger, except for her long, wavy braids. We hugged.

"Laana, I'm so happy to see you," Taylor said, pulling back so I could see her face. "I'm sorry to hear about what happened."

"Thanks," I said.

"If there's anything I can do –"

"I know."

"What brings you in here today?"

"Actually, about that… do you need any help? Any CDs that

need shelving, anything?"

"You know what, I definitely could use your help."

"I'm so glad to hear that. I really need —"

"A distraction?"

"Something to do while I'm home."

★ ★ ★

I guess I expected to see ghosts everywhere, walking around Clifton. People I used to know, people I forgot. Instead, I saw ghosts in my toys and books. In glimpses of memories I had of myself at ten, twelve, thirteen, fifteen, sixteen, seventeen, wandering through the house, looking for some book or album, putting up and taking down posters. I found those posters; I still see the marks they left on the walls. I put them back up to hide the unfaded patches of paint.

Sometimes I catch myself walking around the house, or glancing at a spine on the bookshelf, a blade of glass on the other side of the window, an old mug on the counter, or maybe the light is streaming in through my window at the right angle and intensity and suddenly I've collided with myself five or ten years ago. And I'm afraid of all the same things.

★ ★ ★

"She drowned in the sea," Nadia, a friend of Hena's, said.

"The sea?" I said. "Clifton is landlocked."

"Sorry, I meant lake," she said.

"Which lake? I don't know any."

"In the park."

"With the fountain?"

"No. The one on the other end. With the ducks."

"Oh, I always thought that was a pond."

"That's where she drowned."

"Can't you stand in it? I'm pretty sure someone fell in at

some point and was fine."

"That's what I heard."

"So, Carolyn drowned in the duck pond in the park? Was it an accident, or on purpose?"

"I don't know. All I remember is some kids found her body the next day."

★ ★ ★

The way ghost stories, or horror movies, or scary fiction work is by making you use your imagination to fill in the gaps. There's so much suspense, so few details. There's always a blank, a delay before an explanation, a pause between knowing that there's something there and finding out what it is. And in that time, you come up with something so scary the actual threat won't compare. Whatever you invent is worse, which is why they hold off on telling you until the end. I used to finish horror movies and breathe a sigh of relief. If you ever encounter someone you think is a good storyteller, they owe you credit. You did a lot of heavy lifting.

★ ★ ★

"I'm always scared I'm gonna die in some horribly stupid way," Amara said. "Like a piece of toast is gonna get stuck in the toaster and I try to fish it out with a fork and electrocute myself in the process. And then when everyone asks how I died they'll be like, 'Oh, she stuck a fork in a toaster,' and at my funeral they'll say, 'She died making toast, which wasn't even a thing she loved'."

"That's elaborate," I said, age fourteen. "And specific."

"It doesn't have to be toast," she shrugged.

"So, you're not afraid of all death, just a certain kind?"

"Yeah, I think that's it. I think if I died of cancer or old age, I'd be happy with that."

"I don't know, I feel like that's more of a preference than a fear."

"Are you afraid of dying?"

"No, I've never been. I guess it just… missed me."

★ ★ ★

It's not an obsession with death. At least I don't think it is. At least not the way we normally think about death. Not the sadness of it. Not loss. Not the biology of it. Not what happens to the body in the ground after it's been there for years, not how the skin and bones transform as they're broken down by the earth.

No, I think about death as a fact. Not as a thing to be running towards, or away from, or because of, or in spite of. As a predetermined outcome. You can't dispute it's coming. It's the one inevitable truth of life, and that level of predictability isn't afforded anywhere else. I am not wishing for my death, but I don't want to live forever. I am comforted by the fact that one day it will end.

I don't think of how I'm going to die, although I'm terrified it's going to be some minor oversight. Some totally avoidable mistake. Some pedestrian mess-up that otherwise would have been a banal fluke, but one that proved fatal in my case.

I think a lot about how I'll live afterwards. I think of what I'll leave behind. If I've made any contributions, done anything which brings me to the attention of strangers. Which belongings go to which friends, who will be close with me at the time. And how they'll all remember me. If it'll be bits and pieces, or the whole. At my funeral and memorial service, will all of their memories be obscured by a search for examples of my kindness, generosity, and what they'll no doubt call my "bright spirit," despite all the evidence to the contrary, or will someone be annoyed, will someone have something awful I said to them once playing on a loop in their head, unable to get it out? Will they shake their head while a relative speaks, trying to forget, to think better of me in death? Will someone remember a time I let them down, a time I frustrated them, will someone think of me as completely ordinary? Will someone suddenly remember that I owed them money? Or forgot to return a book? Will they form new characters from selected memories? Will time cherry-pick the moments that determine the versions of me that live on?

I think about this a lot with the people I know, especially when I haven't seen them in a while. What does Amara think of me? Sairah? Am I the person she remembers from high school, or the one now, and can she ever separate them? Which person did Faiz think he was meeting in the store – his friend from fifth grade, the face in the hallway in high school, or someone completely different? Sometimes my parents say a thing about me that hasn't been true for five years and it feels like I'm more than one person. It's almost like they've replaced me. Or they haven't let the current me replace the old me.

And yet, I'd rather be completely forgotten.

★ ★ ★

"Did you ever hear about the ghost of Carolyn Hayward?" I asked Taylor as I helped her re-shelve CDs at the record store. I handed her an album. There were four people on the cover – only one of them was still alive. When I listened to the songs, it felt like hearing a ghost.

"Did I?" she laughed. "I've heard so many versions they've got tangled in my head."

"There are a lot of stories, all with different endings," I said.

"You know, I always thought my parents told us about Carolyn to keep us from playing near her house," Taylor said. "I wonder how many other ghost stories were just meant to scare kids out of trouble."

"Yeah, but it's not like it worked." After a pause, I asked, "What was the weirdest one? Or the one you liked the most?"

"Weirdest was that she was poisoned in a blood feud between her family and one of the others. I liked all the ones where she faked her death and ran away to become an actress or something."

"Which family had the blood feud?"

"One of the really old ones. The Emersons maybe? Or the Matthews?"

"How long has your family been here?"

"Longer than them. We got here long before the Haywards."

But no plaques, or statues, no names in the history books.

★ ★ ★

"What stories do you think they'll tell about us when we're dead?" I asked. "I think I just want to fade away into obscurity. Be forgotten."

"I don't want to forget you," Sairah said.

"Who says you're gonna outlive me?" I replied.

She shrugged. "I always thought I wanted to be taught in schools. I never wanted to achieve any fame or recognition in my lifetime and that way I would avoid all the pressure. But then eventually, my work will be read and respected and students will be groaning about having my name on their syllabi and debating what I meant when I open some story with a thunderstorm and relating facts of my life to the obviously arbitrary details of my work."

"So, you want to live on after your death?"

"I think I just want to separate part of my life for when I'm dead."

★ ★ ★

I don't think ghosts are nearly as scary or as powerful or as persistent or as annoying as the things that actually haunt you. That thing you thought you should write down, but you decided not to anyway and you forgot it and now you can't remember it. It's worse than just forgetting because you're aware you've forgotten and you know there's something you can't remember, but you think that if you think hard enough it'll come back to you, it'll just magically appear, just materialise in your brain.

Then there are the things you remember. The things you said you would do and you didn't. The items uncrossed on your to-do list. The things you wish you hadn't done. The things you wish you had said. The things you wish you could take back. The memories you wanted but never had.

These things chill you, fill you with dread — sometimes you'll be reminded by a word, an image, you'll hear a voice, you'll have a flashback. You may shudder or wince. You'll be filled with a sense of loathing, displeasure, shame, before you even know what's happening. And then you decide to figure out why that thing is causing you so much misery. And you follow the thread of memories and associations until you remember what it was. And you're even angrier at yourself than before because you decided to access the memory fully, to feel the emotions completely, and now you feel worse.

But you couldn't just have that cloud of dread hanging around you, clinging like vapour to hair and wool, you needed a solid moment, you didn't want the feeling of almost remembering, you wanted to do it wholly.

If they wanted to make a movie about something truly frightening, they'd make one about regret.

★ ★ ★

"Okay, so I've been doing research," I announced. Both of my parents looked up from their textbooks. "And by research, I mean I've been asking everyone I know. And everyone heard a different version of Carolyn Hayward's story. And they all think she died in some violent way instead of from a disease."

"That's not how the story went," Mom said.

"What? That's what you told me. All the time. Before bed," I said.

"You were telling her ghost stories before bed?" Dad asked.

"I had to change the ending because, as you point out," Mom gestured at Dad, "it was unsuitable for children."

"So, what was the actual story?"

"The version I heard was that she killed herself," Mom said. "Drowned in the bath."

"Dad," I said. "What did you hear?"

"That she died of old age," he said. "People just sensationalised it."

Chapter 2

I made the mistake of letting Dad pick the music.

"I haven't heard this in years," I groaned from the passenger seat.

"You've been missing out," he said.

"I really hate how you have to drive everywhere here."

"It must be so nice. In the city. With your extensive public transport and short distances. You can hop on the subway or even walk."

"Why are the distances so huge here?"

"It gives you more time to listen to music," he said. "You've always wanted to get out of the suburbs."

"Right now, I want out of this metal trap."

"I guess home has always felt like a trap to you."

"That's not what I meant."

"That's what you said. Not now, but before."

This is the downside to spending time with people who have literally known you for decades. They all remember an earlier version of you. They remember things you've said or done that even you don't remember (or want to remember) and choose the most uncomfortable moment to catch you off-guard with some only partially true story.

I had said as much, but it never actually felt like a trap, more like a waiting room. Everything's so quiet and so far. The silence swallows you whole, you can't fill the chasms between two places with anything. You're engulfed by your own thoughts. You're forced to face truths you thought you buried. Until finally, you're able to get out and move on.

It would be so much easier if I could just forget all those things I said or other people said to me or things I did. Instead, I have to carry them around with me, all the time, this great weight.

Maybe that's what's so scary about ghosts. The past is not the past. It can come back to you. You can live it again.

* * *

A girl in my second-grade class — I don't remember her name, she only lived in Clifton briefly — said she had seen Carolyn once, floating above her bed when she woke up from a bad dream. Carolyn scowled and screamed at her and then dissipated, evaporated into the ceiling, into the air, back to where she came from, fading away into the night, into the nightmares of little girls who couldn't fall back to sleep, who dreamed too intensely. I couldn't help thinking about how terrible it must have been to wake up from a nightmare and see a ghost, as if the nightmare was a warm-up, but couldn't prepare you for how awful real life is. As if you were scared, only to immediately have that fear pale in comparison. Out of the frying pan and into the fire.

* * *

One night, at approximately 1:30 am, in the midst of a late-night YouTube deep-dive interspliced with old music videos, nothing but my old string lights and the cool glow of my laptop screen lighting up my room, I ended up on a creepypasta titled "The Ghost of Creek Hill".

Carolyn of Creek Hill is a popular urban legend.

"Suburban," I muttered.

She was murdered at the age of twenty-three. She was studying to be a nurse, but never practiced. On the night of January 17th, 1849, she went to bed at around 11:11 pm. She turned off all the lights and closed all the doors and windows. She fell asleep quietly, peacefully, alone. A couple of hours later, an intruder snuck in at roughly 1:23 am. Nobody knows how or why they entered the house. The intruder walked up the steps to the top floor, went into Carolyn's bedroom and stabbed her twice in the chest as she slept. She was dead in five minutes.

The murderer slipped out of the house unseen. The police could find no trace of the intruder the next morning. Carolyn's murderer was never caught. She became a ghost to find her killer and bring them to justice.

Here are areas where she's been sighted:
Clifton Hospital
Creek Hill Cemetery, aka Creep Hill
Waybrook Elementary
Underneath the Wishing Bridge at Grosvenor Park

I laughed at the idea of Carolyn's ghost hiding under the bridge as Sairah and I walked by, gossiping, yelling or laughing. I wonder what she could have heard, and what she would have thought of us. Of me.

I texted Sairah: Hey, wanna go check out the house on Creek Hill tomorrow?

She replied: As fun as that sounds, I'm hanging with some friends.

I jokingly texted back: You have friends??? Who are not me???

She reacted with the laughing option and wrote back: Lol I had to make some since you abandoned me.

My turn to laugh digitally. I replied: When can you fit me into your busy social calendar?

She texted: Thursday, sorry.

I wrote: Oh wow it really is busy.

She replied: Sorry but we'll definitely make time to hang!

I texted Faiz.

★ ★ ★

"Why'd you ask me to meet you here?" Faiz said.

"Do you remember the story of the ghost of Carolyn Hayward?" I asked.

"Do you realise how creepy this sounds?" he replied.

"What's the version you heard?" I asked.

"Drowned in the bath."

"On purpose or by accident?"

"By accident, I think."

"Interesting," I said softly, pulling out my notebook and writing it down.

He lowered his head, trying to catch my gaze, but I was still bent over my notebook. "You want to tell me what's going on?"

I slammed the book shut. "You know I've had like twelve people tell me that story and no one can agree on how she died. They all have different explanations."

"I'm sure since she was a nurse or something it was an infection. Unless she wasn't a nurse?"

"Oh no, that's been corroborated. Although I haven't found anything to prove that other people lived in the house with her. Do you know anybody who might know anything about this? Local history enthusiasts or something?"

"Hey, you know I haven't seen you in, like, six years? Don't you want to talk about how college was? Work? Don't you want to know how my gap year was?"

I didn't know how to respond. I stood there, silent for a few moments before I finally managed, "Well, yeah, of course."

"But you want to know about the ghost more."

I didn't say anything.

Faiz sighed and looked at me. "Come on. I have something to show you."

★ ★ ★

"Do you remember fifth grade?" Faiz asked, as we pulled up to his house.

"What a question," I replied. "I remember parts of fifth grade. Very few parts. I don't remember any of fourth grade. Third grade I remember pretty well."

"Okay, do you remember the history project we had to do in fifth grade?" Faiz said.

"You're gonna have to be more specific."

"We had to research a historical figure by reading a book about them and present a summary of what we learned." He looked at me. "I chose Creepy Carolyn."

I looked back at him blankly.

"Wait, you seriously don't remember?" he asked. I shook my head. "I thought that's why you wanted to see me. Why'd you text me then?"

"You're the only person I know here who's not Sairah," I said. "And Sairah had plans. Also, I wanted to catch up."

"Not buying that last part."

"I thought this would be a fun thing to do! Oh come on, this beats the whole how-are-you-I'm-doing-great charade. Nobody ever tells the truth or says what they really mean. You know how I am. I know how you are. And we didn't even have to tell each other."

"A ghost hunt is a stretch, though."

"Is it? We're kind of like ghosts to each other, aren't we? Memories, but foreign, otherworldly," I said, mock-wistfully.

He smiled slightly. "Speaking of foreign, on one of my gap years I went to Italy."

I groaned. "Oh, don't tell me you've grown into one of those people!"

"It's always, 'Who'd you turn into?' That's always the question. Everyone was a good kid. But 'Who did you become?'"

"I wasn't a good kid. I was kind of a brat. I hope nobody remembers who I was."

"I remember exactly who you were."

"Which is why you were so thrilled to see me."

"You weren't a brat. A little bit of a know-it-all. But thank God you've outgrown that."

★ ★ ★

"I totally remember this place!" I said, as we climbed up to the attic.

"Yeah, we permanently scarred Amara by making her watch *The Ring* up here in the seventh grade. I don't think she ever forgave me."

He moved some old suitcases out of the way so he could reach the bottom shelf of a bookcase. He pulled out a red binder and flipped through it. Some pages fell out. I bent to pick them up. He slammed the binder down, pried the rings open and lifted out the report. He handed it to me.

"Check the bibliography," he said. "Always –"

I chimed in. "Cite your sources," we said in unison.

"Some things never leave you," Faiz said.

"Yeah, why do you still have this?"

"Same old Laana, asking too many questions."

"Hey, you were a fan when I was stalling in science class. Why are you hating now?"

"I grew up. I changed. I don't listen to the same music I did in high school."

"I do."

"Have you wondered why you need to do all of this," he gestured around. "Research? On someone you didn't even know."

"I think you know why."

"But do you?"

"It's obvious, isn't it?"

★ ★ ★

I walked straight through the doors of the library and set down my old library card and driver's license, still in mint condition, on the front desk.

"I need everything you have on local history," I said.

The librarian surveyed me coolly. "Laana Hashmi, still barging in here the same way you did when you were six."

I shuddered, feeling a creeping sense of embarrassment. "Sorry, I —"

She smiled and started walking. "Come on. I know how important those books must be."

★ ★ ★

"I hope you're not planning on moving back here," Dad said, when he saw all the boxes.

"You should be so lucky," I replied, setting the last of them on the floor in the hallway.

"Laans, don't leave them in the way," Mom called from the kitchen. I nodded even though she couldn't see me, and picked the box up.

"Then who – or what – is moving in here?" he said, surveying the cardboard cubes littering the hallway.

"Library books," I said, walking up the stairs.

"Why?" he said hesitantly, following me to my room.

"I am trying to figure out what actually happened to Carolyn Hayward," I said, putting down a box.

"It's just a myth. You won't find answers, because there's nothing there to find."

Death is, in addition to other things, a physical fact. There are all of these details that need to be attended to, like purchasing a coffin and figuring out where you'll be buried and what type of grave you'll have and what will be on the gravestone. And what happens to your home, your belongings, all the physical aspects of your life. And then there are things like bank accounts and legal paperwork. You always leave a trace.

"Someone has to have lived there. It's a house," I said. I sat on the floor and opened one of the boxes. I pulled out a stack of documents and shuffled through them.

Dad sat next to me and reached into the box. "You know, this is how we used to do research," he said, pulling out an old, thin history book.

"And you couldn't Google. And it was impossible to find out about new bands because there was no YouTube or Spotify. And you couldn't text or call your friends, you had to send carrier pigeons and decide on a place and time and hope everyone ended up there and you weren't just going to see a black-and-white silent film by yourself."

He laughed. "And no digitised library systems, either. You'd have to look it up in the catalogue. And then search the shelves."

"And read so much microfilm it would send you straight to the optician's office."

"It's weird to think that you leave so much of a record behind."

"It's worse now. Imagine every email, text and photo."

"And still, it's nothing if you didn't know the person."

★ ★ ★

I was at home alone that night. My parents had gone out to dinner with some of their friends. Another unexpected challenge of going home was dealing with the fact that, for the duration of my stay, my parents had a busier social life than I did.

When I was alone at night, I would hear all these noises. I somehow became more acutely aware of sounds I'd never heard before, as if my parent's absence had illuminated them. It was times like these I wished I believed in ghosts, instead of worrying about intruders – humans, insects, or rodents.

One time I woke up from a nap thinking I had dreamt a bird had crashed into a window, and then found one in the house.

I wonder if the sounds I was hearing now were real – the

wind, the birds, potentially a tree branch falling, a neighbour yelling, maybe we do have a rat problem – or if they were imagined. If my brain expected my parents to be here and was just filling them in for my ears.

I wonder what they heard when I left home – the sounds they thought I made or the silence.

* * *

I had found our *Poltergeist* DVD when Dad and I had gone through records in the attic a few days before. I got about twenty minutes through it until I felt too scared. I paused it, then sat on the couch wrapped in a fleece blanket, trying to decide whether I could be brave enough to go on until my parents came back from dinner.

It was still on pause when my mom sat down next to me. She hadn't taken off her jacket or shoes.

"Is this *Poltergeist*?" she asked. "I love this movie! Why didn't you tell me you were going to watch it? I can't believe we still have this." I was silent. She turned to look at me. "It's less scary when someone's watching with you."

"You would watch it by yourself," I said.

"And it's barely scary without the music." She turned off the volume. "I used to sneak downstairs and watch movies as a teenager, and I'd have to mute them. Not scary at all."

"As a teenager?"

"This is one of my favourites."

"You're desensitised."

"I'm going to watch this. You can watch with me if you'd like."

"Okay, I'll try to be brave."

"You don't scare easily. You get that from me." Most fears are learned. Small children, like really small, aren't afraid of bugs or dogs or other things. It's only when you tell them to be afraid of them, when you teach them that certain things are dangerous, when they see that someone else is scared of something that they learn to fear those things themselves.

I fell asleep on the couch fifteen minutes later.

★ ★ ★

We had all our best conversations by the river. On top of the old stone bridge. On the stepping stones that created a path across the shallower part. Sitting on the benches beside it in the summer.

The river had also stolen a lot from us. Over the course of my life, it had swallowed up index cards, a single Converse without its twin, bags of chips, a ruler, gloves, sunglasses. I had lost a friendship bracelet Sairah had given me and freaked out. I jumped into the river to search for it and avoided Sairah for three days while I tried to find one that looked just like it, embarrassed that I would let a river come between us.

I say river, but it was a creek. The same creek near Carolyn's house ran through the park as well. But everyone called it a river.

Sairah led the way to the bridge, which was good because I wouldn't be able to navigate what had become of the park. Colourful seesaws and swings had sprung up. They had downsized the existing playground and padded it with that spongy substance that looks like tar, but is a springy, weightless cross between foam and rubber.

"I guess it's for safety?" Sairah said, testing the substance by prodding it with the toe of her boot. "We didn't have any of this stuff and we were fine."

"Yeah, we used to break into the cemetery, tell ghost stories and jump off the top of the playground instead of using the pole," I said with a smile. "Isn't that how you sprained your wrist?"

"No. I broke it on the monkey bars at school."

"Weird. I always thought it happened at the playground that used to be here. That's why I avoided it for so long. I guess I thought it was cursed."

"I'm telling you, as the proud owner of the wrist in question, it was the monkey bars. And you continued using those cursed monkey bars."

"You're a reliable source. But if you think about it, monkey bars are really not that safe."

"Nothing we did was. Or else why would we do it?"

★ ★ ★

I opened *The Founding Families of Connecticut* to chapter eight, titled "The Haywards":

> *The first generation of Haywards were among the early settlers and founders of the town. The second acted as leaders of the town as it continued to expand.*

I remembered as much from my elementary school history classes. I knew that if I ever bothered to look at the rest of the book, it would be the same story for all the other families: they created Clifton and then they ran Clifton.

> *The third generation was quite wealthy and prosperous, and instead turned their attention to philanthropy. They founded the town's first hospital, then called Hayward Hospital.*

It matched up with most of what I'd read. I scanned down to the final, short paragraph:

> *The fourth generation consisted of one member: Carolyn Hayward. She and her parents died in Hayward Manor in 1878 during a malaria outbreak. She never married.*

★ ★ ★

This time on my jog, I kept going after I had finished my loop of the cemetery. I ran out through the gates, onto the sidewalk. I kept running. I ran towards the Hayward compound. I didn't cross the street, instead running across the sidewalk opposite, moving parallel to the house, the gate obscured behind a clump of trees.

The road formed a circle around that island of trees, with the gates to Hayward Manor at one end and me on the other. As I jogged, I caught glimpses of the wrought-iron gate, the lock probably rusted shut after having been kept closed for so long. I wondered if anyone else had wanted to open it. I wondered if anyone had tried.

I saw the edges of the house, looming a distance past the gate. Big and imposing. I thought of Carolyn alone in that huge house, hearing noises and wondering where they were coming from, echoes of footsteps, wondering if anyone had come in there, if she had left any windows open, forgetting things in one room and having to check three or four to find them, thinking the rooms should be filled with people and remembering them there. Seeing memories of her family in each inch of the enormous house. Who knows, maybe she was haunted by something too. Maybe we're all just trapped in a circle of haunting, of remembering and forgetting, of guilt and regret.

★ ★ ★

"How do you think people become ghosts?" Sairah said. "After they die?"

I waited. Sairah normally had an answer prepared.

"I always thought it was having unfinished business," she said.

"Doesn't everyone have unfinished business?" I thought about all the items left unchecked on my to-do list every night before I went to sleep. So many people fear death like a deadline.

After all, everyone could use an extension. In the weeks after my grandmother's death, friends of hers delivered dishes and books they had borrowed months ago and forgot to return.

"I thought you didn't believe in ghosts," Sairah said.

"I wish I did. Then I wouldn't be so scared every time I hear a random noise when I'm alone in the house. Because then I either worry about having to find an exterminator or, worse, spend hours thinking a burglar stole something or there's a murderer hiding in the other room."

"So, you think living things are scarier than dead ones?"

"Not necessarily. The living are just as capable of evil, but not everyone is. Who's to say how ghosts would behave or feel? There are aggressive and mean people and there are kind and generous people."

"You think they're just like every other person? Where's the fun in that?"

"I don't have your sense of imagination."

"Makes it much easier to believe in ghosts."

"I wish I could be more open to things, not just –"

"Facts?"

"Why do we always assume ghosts are going to be malicious? Maybe Carolyn just wants to pass on some medical tips."

"I like to think she's looking out for us."

I looked up at her. "Have you ever seen her?"

"I have seen very few ghosts, and none of them were her."

"Who were they?"

"Nobody I recognised."

"And they weren't evil, were they?"

Sairah shook her head.

"So then why are they always villains?"

"People fear what they don't know. They're scared of anything – or anyone – that's different from what they know."

"Yeah, that sounds right," I scoffed. "But what about ghosts that people know? I would have thought people would want to talk to people they lost."

"Not if they wronged them."

"So, it's guilt?"

"Some ghosts are believed to be out for revenge, or acting violently because something was done to them."

"So, ghosts aren't inherently evil. They're reacting." People don't want to be reminded of what they've done. Or didn't do.

★ ★ ★

From *Women in Medicine*, page 118:

Carolyn Hayward (1851–1889)

Carolyn Hayward was born to Charles and Annabelle Hayward, prominent Connecticut philanthropists. Her parents founded the hospital in her hometown of Clifton, called Hayward Hospital, which was later renamed Clifton Hospital.

Her family was wealthy, so her education was a formality. She didn't need to work, and therefore didn't need to get a professional degree or go to a vocational school. Nevertheless, she decided to go to nursing school, graduating at the top of her class.

She went to work in the hospital her parents founded. She was known for working hard and being dedicated to her patients.

In 1887, after the death of her parents, she took over the management of the hospital.

She died in 1889, at the age of thirty-seven, likely from complications relating to pneumonia.

★ ★ ★

I put on one of the first records Dad had given me when I bought my Crosley in tenth grade. It had been his favourite record when he was fifteen. I started flipping through a book about hospitals in central Connecticut.

Dad stuck his head into the room. "Look at you sorting through research like you don't have other research to do."

"I can't explain it," I said. "I just have to get to the bottom of this."

"I'm happy you're suddenly interested in this town. I thought you hated it here."

"I just hated everything. Nobody likes being a teenager anywhere."

"I'm also surprised you're listening to this. Finally, you've grown up."

"You haven't. This was your favourite album when you were a teenager."

"And it still is."

"You're stuck in the past."

"Laana, you need to stop thinking of everybody as stuck."

* * *

You exist in multiple forms – physical, metaphysical, professional, legal – and you will eventually stop existing in all these ways. Or almost all. But they all end a little differently. Your family has to obtain a death certificate. You stop breathing. Your work is published afterwards. You smile in old photographs. You talk in videos. You laugh in memories. People might still hear you in their homes, see you in picture frames or in mirrors.

You die in all those ways, but not always at the same time. In a legal sense, if you don't get a death certificate, you can live on past your body. There will be people to remember you, until there aren't. There will be photographs of you passed down until they're stuck in old albums, forgotten on the back of a shelf somewhere.

Even Carolyn left a trace. Her name was in newspapers, her handwriting in hospital records, her face in portraits. She would have bought things and got receipts. She sent letters. She kept a diary. They persisted past her. Would they outlive me?

★ ★ ★

"It looks... smaller than I remember," Sairah said.

The bushes and shrubs looked like cardboard cut-outs in the harsh, white streetlight glare. You couldn't make out any of the writing on the gravestones. The gate had been left ajar. Nobody had bothered to close it fully.

"No respect for the dead," I said.

"Or the living," Sairah replied.

I opened the gate and whipped out my flashlight. Sairah followed dutifully.

I guess I was expecting something different, but it was as disappointing at night as it was in the daytime. It was pitch black. Headstones and small statues sprung up as I swung my flashlight at the dark blanket of nothing surrounding us. Everything seemed dull and two-dimensional. I think some part of me expected Gothic mist and a bone-cutting chill. But it was summer, and I was starting to sweat in my denim jacket as I made my way through the rows of graves. None of it felt real.

"I keep forgetting there are actual people here," Sairah said.

"It sometimes just feels like rocks and names," I said. "And not even names at that." I shone my flashlight on a grave where the text had faded in parts, worn down through the years. Whoever was once there now half-erased.

"Where's Daadi?" Sairah asked. I pointed to the far end of the cemetery. We both looked in that direction, but neither of us moved.

We stood among the graves in silence for a few moments. Then I walked over to an empty patch of grass and sat down. Sairah followed. I looked around.

"Does it feel any different?" Sairah asked.

"Not really," I said. "It's always felt like this. Like it's supposed to feel like something, and it doesn't." I thought about the stones, the grass, the trees, the people in the ground, their souls, here or elsewhere, and thought of how little changed from day to day, year to year, century to century.

"Where are your grandparents buried?" I asked. I knew they weren't here. I hadn't seen their names.

"In Karachi." I remembered Sairah and her family travelling there after the death of her grandfather – her last remaining grandparent – when we were eight.

I got up and Sairah followed silently. I led her to the giant statue. The sculpture could have been of any woman. It could have been me or Sairah or Hena or my mom or my grand-mother or Taylor or Taylor's aunt. It was so unremarkable, so unrecognisable. It didn't look like any image I had ever seen of Carolyn. When I was younger, I would see her statue in the distance, glinting pale white, and I would think she looked like an angel. But now, older and grey, cracked and speckled, blue in the white beam of the flashlight, she looked cold, worn and weary. I thought that if she came to life she would be exhausted and cynical, hardened and annoyed by all the things she had seen and lived through. Hayward Manor would outlast her. Hayward Hospital had lived more lives than she had.

"That's not what she looks like," Sairah said.

I looked at her. "How do you know what she looks like?"

"It's just not how I imagined her."

"Same here."

"I'd hate for my statue to be so off."

"You think people are going to build statues of you?"

She turned and smiled at me. "You think they won't?"

★ ★ ★

A part of me believed that when you die, you disappear. It's true in some ways – the person that was is no longer there: mentally, physically, personality-wise. But all their belongings remain, their house and room and clothes look the same, still hanging up in the cupboards as if the deceased is miraculously going to climb out of their grave, walk home from the cemetery, take them off the hanger and put them back on. Instead, you're left with everything they had and you have to make all the decisions about what happens to them, literally dismantling the person that was.

★ ★ ★

That Sunday, Dad and I sat in the attic sorting through old vinyl records. His keep pile was sprawled on the rug near us, while mine was empty.

"There's nothing here worth saving," I said.

"Your sensibilities are unrefined," he said.

"Sensibilities is a gendered term."

He considered what I said. "It is. What I meant is that you haven't developed taste."

"No, I just haven't developed *your* taste in music."

"The right taste in music."

I shot him a look. "Why do you have so many of these?"

"Well, one of the great things about the suburbs is all the storage space. Not like your tiny, overpriced city apartments."

"Or you've just stayed in one place too long. You haven't done the pre-move sorting and discarding that makes you question why you decided to have material possessions in the first place." I stopped. "How many people in this town would you say have been living in the same houses for the last twenty years?"

"That's not a statistic I have off of the top of my head, but −"

"But it's a lot, right? Most of the houses are old. There hasn't been a lot of development. We like our old houses. No one moves. Everyone my age lived in the same house from when they were born until they left for college."

"Some longer. The Matthews have been in that house since the beginning of Clifton."

"And the Hayward House is still up."

"Not for long."

"It's never coming down."

"Because of the ghost."

"I wonder why she doesn't want to leave."

"Maybe there's someone at City Hall who doesn't want to see the house gone. Or is worried about upsetting Carolyn."

"I wonder why more people don't leave."

"Maybe – and I know this is hard for you to believe – some people like Clifton and want to stay here."

"Ghost or no ghost – this town is cursed."

★ ★ ★

From *Medical Connecticut*:

> *Clifton Hospital, currently a children's hospital, was originally founded as Hayward Hospital in 1841 by the Hayward family. Carolyn Hayward, who graduated at the top of her class from the Connecticut College of Nursing, converted the east wing of the hospital into a clinic for children. Since then, the hospital has had an emphasis on caring for infants and children, so much so that it is now a children's hospital.*

I turned to the chapter titled "Connecticut College of Nursing":

> *The Connecticut College of Nursing was founded in 1833. The program took roughly eighteen months and was seen as one of the most rigorous nursing programs in the Northeast. It was highly competitive, and students were ranked. It was even selective in its admissions process.*
>
> *The college produced many notable alumni, including Grace Shepherd, who founded the Boston College of Nursing, and Carolyn Hayward, who went on to manage her family's hospital in Clifton, Connecticut, and started a children's wing there.*
>
> *The college closed in 1908.*

★ ★ ★

The next day, after a lap around the cemetery, I jogged right up to the gates of Hayward Manor.

When we had just learned how to ride our bikes, we used to cycle by the house all the time. We liked to do laps in the ring of the road that looped around the patch of trees, careful to not go too close to the gate, for fear of the ghost. I guess nobody was taking care of the house then, because I remember the gate being covered in vines so thick you couldn't tell if there really was a house behind it.

We never saw the house, even when they cleared up all the foliage. Taking a break from my run to peer through the now bare bars, I couldn't see anything. The gate was easily twice my height, flanked by stone columns. It was built to last centuries. From books, I knew the Georgian-style house was three stories tall and from photos I knew it had twelve-pane windows. But I had never seen it up close. And didn't think I ever would.

I did see the stretch of driveway leading up to the house, with oak trees lining the path, and for a second it felt like I was staring into a different time period, shut out, unable to go in. I checked the lock, the size of an orange and almost the same colour with rust.

I felt disappointed, like I did the first time I visited the cemetery at night: calm, normal, neutral if anything at all. Not scared, I didn't feel any lingering presence.

I felt alone.

★ ★ ★

"It's so weird that they're going to get rid of Hayward Manor," I said. "That huge house, just gone."

"It's never going to happen," Dad said. "If they were going to do it, they would have done it years ago."

I wondered if it was like that item that sat on your to-do list without ever getting done or crossed off, forgotten, overlooked for months. Almost as if you never put it on, like you never meant to get it done and you never would.

The fact that the house was supposed to come down became as permanent as the house itself.

"That house is huge, though," Dad said. "It looked incredible."

We sat in silence for a second. Then something occurred to me. "How did you know that? No one's allowed near the house."

"Oh, you used to be able to visit the compound," he said. "They kept the gates open and even school trips would visit. You weren't allowed inside the house, but you could walk around the grounds."

"Or run," Mom said.

"What was it like?" I asked.

"Big, old stone house," Dad said. "It looked just like the photographs."

"Which photographs?" I asked.

"From the textbooks," he said.

"Do you still have those, by any chance?" I asked.

"I didn't want to keep my old textbooks any more than you do. But I'm sure some of them made their way to Brooks' by now. You might be able to find the pictures online," Dad said.

"You also took some good photos," Mom said. "If I remember correctly."

"You did?" I asked.

"Your dad was really into photography for a while," Mom said.

"It was just a phase," he said. "I never stuck with it."

"But do you still have the photos?"

"I'll find them for you, Laana," Dad said, getting up and walking upstairs.

★ ★ ★

Three hours later, he came into my room with an old shoebox. He set it in front of me on my desk. Neither of us said a word. I looked through it, picking up the old plastic film canisters. They were useful growing up. We used to store everything from earrings to medicine in them, our own travel sets. Plastic lasts forever, but they stopped making them. I always wondered what we'd do, how we'd get more if we needed them, what we would do instead, if we would even miss them. And here were three of them, empty, not being used for anything. I took them out and set them on my desk in a row.

Then I started going through the photos. There were some from my lifetime. Family vacations. Birthday parties. Me as a baby. Then I got to the ones that predated me. My parents on trips before I was born. Dad getting his PhD. Mom getting her PhD a year earlier.

Then we were even further back in time to when Mom and Dad were in college when they first moved to Clifton. It was, unsurprisingly, more or less the same town, in faded, muted colours. There were the gates of Hayward Manor, wide open. The grass was thick and overgrown; the path leading up to the house was so pale it gleamed. There were people on it. I found it hard to believe.

A group of kids in brightly coloured shirts stood in front of the house. The house was pale white with black windows and doors. The front door was large, as I thought it would be, but there was an ornate border around it. The grills on the windows looked like lace. It was almost too perfect; it would easily lend itself to a ghost story.

I picked up another picture. There was someone standing on the front porch while others ran around the garden.

"There's your mom." He pointed at a flash of black hair in the corner of one photo. It looked like she was running to the back of the house. "She was never scared of ghosts. Kind of like you, but you've taken it to another level. But then again, you always loved mystery books and solving puzzles."

"If you mean Clue," I said, shuffling through the rest of the photos. "I know you used to cheat when you were dealing the cards."

"What are you talking about? I would never cheat."

"Most parents lose on purpose for their kids. But that's still cheating, in a way."

"I never lost on purpose. And I didn't cheat. You won most of the time."

I flicked through the photos, this time going forward through time to the first decade of my life. In the corner, I thought I saw Sairah. I did see Sairah, aged eight, but I also saw what I thought was present-day Sairah somehow finding her way into the past. I held up the photo, trying to look at it more closely. I always thought I resembled both my parents. Well, actually, both of my grandmothers, but my parents looked a little like their mothers, just because most people often do in some way or other. But Sairah was the exact copy of her mother. Sairah's parents had photos of themselves as kids on their table, and as a child I thought they were photos of Sairah and always wondered where I was.

"Sairah's mom," Dad said.

"She looks just like her," I said.

"It's funny because Hena looks nothing like either of her parents."

"I think that's normal, actually. It's weird that I look so much like both of you."

"I always thought you looked a lot like your mother, not that much like me."

I looked down at the box, filled with partial copies of the same faces, duplicated again and again. "Thanks for the photos," I said.

As he turned to leave, I suddenly remembered something; "Dad," I called out. He stopped. "I was always the one who dealt the cards."

★ ★ ★

"How did people feel about Carolyn when she was alive?" Sairah asked.

I tilted my head. "I've never thought about it," I said.

"I mean, do you think there was a reason everyone acted like she was evil?" Sairah said.

"You think she did something?" I asked.

"Not necessarily." She paused and stared off for a minute.

"I do sometimes think she was being punished for something." For accomplishing too much. For being too powerful, too ambitious, too strong, too good at her job. For being too different. Not normal enough. Just a little strange, unusual, a bit weird.

"You know how I took that trip to Savannah last year and did those ghost tours? There are all these towns that are so haunted, but they also have, like, these really problematic and traumatic histories, like –"

"They were haunted even without the ghosts."

"Like the ghosts were some reflection of that."

"So, the question is what's haunting us?"

"It's not like anything interesting happens here anyway."

"That's a good question. How does someone become a ghost story? What if there's no reason?"

"Then we could become ghost stories."

"A bad reputation is worse than doing something bad." It was something my grandmother used to say, and my mom too. I think it was an old Urdu saying. "Or being bad."

Chapter 3

While reorganizing CDs at Taylor's record shop, I came across an old album I was obsessed with in ninth grade. "I can't believe I used to like this," I said.

"You're supposed to feel that way," Taylor said.

I looked at her, puzzled.

"Haven't you grown up by now?"

I laughed. "Not in the slightest."

"I think embarrassment is a good thing."

"I would love to have that perspective."

"Okay, maybe more like a sign? That you've grown and changed, hopefully for the better."

I stared at the album artwork. "But are you sure it's growth? I feel like some people just decide not to like things to show they've changed. Or maybe this music is just associated with something I don't want to think about."

Taylor considered what I said.

I continued, "Doesn't everything ruin music? Doesn't it always remind you of something? I heard a song the other day and it reminded me of junior year of college." It doesn't matter that it was my roommate's favourite song, or we played it at our college graduation party, or I played it all the time when I moved into my apartment in the city, or I used to listen to it on the way to class and, in my mind, it's attached itself to all these things. How can you ever hear that song for what it was when it just reminds you of everything you've been through?

There are also songs I only like because they evoke good memories. A song playing on the radio in the taxi on the way back from a concert. An annoying pop song playing at the end of a good movie. A friend who really loved a song you normally wouldn't listen to.

Then there are the mundane associations: the ringtones, the alarms, the songs you would listen to when you woke up, or on the subway, or while folding laundry, or doing the dishes.

I suddenly remembered a conversation Taylor and I had years ago.

"All art is based on what came before it. It's referring to everything else and if not, it's building off it or inspired by it," Taylor said.

"There are always precedents," I said.

★ ★ ★

I sat on one of the benches by the creek writing down a list of all the stories I remembered hearing: fire, disappearance, natural death, pneumonia, malaria, scarlet fever, cholera, tuberculosis, typhus, unspecified illness, drowning by accident, drowning on purpose, premeditated murder, manslaughter, murder by accident, poison, suicide (hanging), suicide by other means. It was almost every way you could think of dying at that period in history. Some of them I had heard more than once, some three times, but none significantly more than others. So many ways you could go.

I stared at the creek for a few minutes. It looked more violent than usual, restless instead of calm. I could see ripples moving quickly, like it was alive. As I turned to go, I thought I saw someone out of the corner of my eye. For a split second, I hoped it was Carolyn. I was close enough to her house.

I turned to look. It was my reflection in the water.

★ ★ ★

Sairah and I were walking through the cemetery in broad daylight. The section we were in had huge headstones with big ornate carvings, and they were spaced out, not crowded and uniform like the others.

"What do you want your gravestone to say?" Sairah asked.

"I don't know," I said. "That's way too much pressure. Something literally set in stone that will outlive you that you can never change? No thanks." We walked a few more steps. "You?"

"Maybe if I have some unfinished work or, like, a really good line or title or something, we could slap it on there."

"In the event I do outlive you, do you still want me to destroy all your drafts?"

"Oh, definitely. Burn it all – every notebook, Word file, Post-it and scrap of paper – anything unpublished shouldn't survive me. I can't think what people would do with that."

I laughed. "But after we pick an epitaph."

"Yeah, you go through everything, pick something to go on my gravestone, then torch it."

"What? You can't give me that responsibility!"

"It's just one line."

I looked around at the graves, trying to see what others had chosen to write on their headstones.

"All the names in this section…" I said, scanning the inscriptions. "They're not like ours. They're white."

Sairah shrugged. "We didn't come until later."

"I haven't seen a single gravestone from this century over here. The latest one was from 1930. Who's even buried here?"

"Prominent founding families or whatever."

"They're the ones who get statues and plaques and… ghosts."

"There's no record, no permanence to us."

"It's like we were never here. If you walked through the cemetery, you would think it's all people like this. This doesn't represent Clifton." I looked at Sairah. "It's like we don't get to have a history."

★ ★ ★

I remember being fascinated the first time I heard about the butterfly effect. Small things that make a difference. It made for a good story. It sounded too good to be true. Insignificant moments or decisions you made long ago that led you to this precise moment, this exact set of circumstances. The important moments aren't really important. But the small moments are, and the bigger ones wouldn't have happened without them. It's hard to tell what's important. It's impossible to know when you're making the decision that could change everything.

★ ★ ★

Some people's ghost encounters seem relatively mundane: things we would chalk up to gravity, or absentmindedness, or carelessness – not arranging the books properly so that one of them falls, forgetting where you put something, stacking items precariously. And I always thought the idea that it was a ghost trying to communicate – rather than you not paying enough attention – was nice, if only because it absolved you of a little blame. In any case it was the more interesting explanation, the one that made you feel less alone.

"I like the idea of Carolyn watching over Clifton," I said. "Protecting us."

"She's been protecting us for a while," Sairah said. "When I broke my wrist, when you were out for two weeks in the seventh grade with the flu. I had no idea she was the one who pushed for the hospital to focus on children. And we act like she's causing problems."

"We were so quick to villainise her," I said quietly.

"Some people are so scared of the past."

"The past never stays in the past." I paused and we took a few steps in silence. "It always haunts me."

"You being here has made me question every memory of my childhood."

"That's the weird thing. College feels like a dream. It seemed to drag on forever when I was going through it, but once it was over it was like it never happened. It doesn't feel real. That was four whole years of my life." I continued. "But other things are so painfully real. None of my memories of Clifton feel like a dream. They're all so vivid and they're always with me. They're always alive. Every moment you wish you could take back. Every moment you wish you could change. Every moment you want to go back and live for a little while longer. It would be easier to forget they ever happened, but you're constantly thinking about them." I took a breath. "If you're scared of the past, you're allowing yourself to be haunted forever." And the weird thing is, when I go back to the city, this will feel like a dream and that will be my reality.

★ ★ ★

"I asked my brother," Faiz said.

"And?" I asked, not looking up from my laptop.

"She fell off the tower."

Sairah and I looked at each other.

"What tower?" I asked at the same time Sairah said, "We don't have a tower," in an exasperated tone.

"That's what he said," Faiz shrugged, picking up his sandwich.

"You didn't think to ask him what he was talking about?" Sairah asked.

He put down his sandwich. "I just assumed he meant the bell tower in City Hall."

I considered it for a second. It was tall. "That's new." Then it occurred to me. "Wait, is City Hall even old enough? There could have been a tower then!"

"I know that look," Sairah said.

"Oh no, I've done it now," Faiz said.

★ ★ ★

I wasn't planning for my funeral, I swear. I was just looking at what the different types of graves are called. The website read like those brochures you get for Invisalign or something. It said things like, "Which grave should you pick for your loved one?" and, "Find a cemetery that's right for your family" and, "Here for all of your post-life solutions." This website listed five different burial options: cremation, in-ground, natural, mausoleum, and lawn crypt.

I found out that the stone tombs aren't actually coffins, but structures placed on top of the plot where the casket lies underground.

The first time I saw all the steps, the time, the tasks, the effort that went into planning a funeral was on some TV show a few years ago. I didn't know it took that much work.

I wasn't home when my parents arranged my grandmother's funeral. They told me all the steps, but I didn't see them doing it. I didn't see what their faces looked like, if they gave any signs of emotion, if they acted happy or sad, if they let others see how they actually felt, if they didn't feel as sad as they thought they should. I didn't see if they were secretly actually annoyed by the technicalities, of all the steps, of how they always call it "solutions" or "needs" no matter what they're trying to sell you, and that you could have gone through loss and grief and be in mourning and at the end of the day you're still just a customer, they're still trying to sell you something, you still have to buy something. Not even grief can spare you that. Some things go on regardless of everything.

★ ★ ★

"You know natural burials are better for the environment?" I said. "And that there are green cemeteries?"

"Laana, you can't just immediately start talking about death when you see people," Faiz said.

I shrugged and took a potato chip off his plate. "Why not? It's the one thing we all have in common."

"That we're all going to die? That's what you want to remind everyone of at the start of a conversation?"

"Don't make it sound so dark."

"Don't make death sound so dark?" he asked, incredulous.

"I just want answers. I want to know what happens. Isn't it weird, literally every person that has ever lived goes through it and yet we know so little about it?"

"I think it's kind of cool we don't know," Sairah said. "The one thing you have to experience for yourself. You have to wait until your time to find out."

"Ugh, I can't wait that long!" I said.

★ ★ ★

My parents had gone to visit some friends. I decided to stay at home and focus on my research. I had to get through a couple of history books about the area and one about nursing. And Faiz had plans. And Sairah was writing.

Since I had the house to myself, I decided to take my books to my parents' study. I put my books on Dad's desk and turned on the light. On one side of the room was Dad's vinyl collection; on the other, Mom's books. Mom was always reading novels. Normally something horror-related. She loved scary movies, Gothic novels, ghost stories, creepy poems – all of it. I ran my finger across the spines, trying to recognise any titles. They were organised in alphabetical order by author. There was some sci-fi, some fantasy. My old book of fairy tales, a book of short stories I bought her for her birthday. There were action thrillers you buy at airports, murder mysteries you get discounted from an out-of-sight shelf in the back of a bookstore. There were a lot of books involving ghosts, but nothing that would help me.

Something stood out: on Dad's shelf there was a vinyl record that belonged to me. I hadn't realised it was missing from my room. I restored it to its rightful place on my shelf, but not before listening to it. It was weird how each word landed now, years later. It was incredible how precisely the lyrics summed up the things I had gone through in the past year. It made me wonder what sixteen-year-old me related to all those lifetimes ago.

The record finished. I pulled out another old one. I had it on repeat the first week of senior year – my last first week of school.

I watched the record spin in the Crosley, the concentric circles like the rings of a tree trunk, spooling outwards. A voice echoed from the past, the words reaching out from years ago and pulling me back to when I was seventeen.

I started to wonder if I had been rehearsing. If I had been going through the motions in preparation for growing up. As if experiencing them then would make them easier in the future.

I was distracted and forgot to skip the song I never liked. A minute into it, I couldn't remember why I had hated it so much.

I listened to it on loop for the rest of the day.

★ ★ ★

I called Devon. It had taken five emails, eight texts and three weeks to schedule this one Zoom call. Devon was now a very successful intellectual property lawyer in Los Angeles, which meant they were very busy. All the time.

"Well, well, well, look at the celebrity lawyer," I said as soon as Devon answered the call.

"Laana, don't act like you don't disappear at the end of every semester. And that you opted to do so many of them. I'm glad we're finally able to talk, though."

"Thanks for the flowers. You can actually be very prompt when needed. You were always there for me. And for Sairah."

"Is it weird being back?"

"It's so strange. It's like nothing has changed. But everything's different. I don't know how to describe it."

"Sairah said you've taken an interest in local history," they said with a grin, raising their eyebrows around the word "interest."

"Yeah. I wanted to ask you what you know about the ghost of Creek Hill."

"Carolyn Hayward. I think she might be my great-great-great-great-aunt or something? Distant. All the founding families are all mixed up now, because there were so few of them."

"Right, I forgot I was talking to Clifton royalty."

"The world's least interesting kingdom."

"But potentially a very interesting set of families. So do you know how Carolyn died?"

"She disappeared one day. And no one knows what happened then."

"That's it?"

"Afraid so. Missing and presumed dead. What, not as exciting as you hoped?"

"It's not as detailed as the other versions I've heard."

"Yeah, well, Clifton loves to embellish."

"Don't we all?"

"Is anyone else still in Clifton? Other than Sairah."

"Faiz is still here."

"I'm sure he and Sairah don't talk as much."

"They're hanging out now."

"That's surprising."

"It was a long time ago!"

"Not long enough."

"We used to all be friends."

"That was a long, long time ago."

★ ★ ★

I watched her die a hundred deaths. Every time I read a line, she died again. Another time, in another way. In another reality, a parallel timeline.

In the same way, I felt like I killed my grandmother every time I mentioned her death, every time I had to tell someone who didn't know and watch her die in their minds. Every time I literally pronounced her dead.

★ ★ ★

From *A Brief History of New England,* page 221:

> *Carolyn Hayward was the daughter of Charles and Annabelle Hayward. She died in a fire in Hayward Manor in 1811. She was unmarried and had no children.*

★ ★ ★

"So, what did we learn today?" Sairah asked, fake-cheery, as if she was talking to a child.

"Nothing because about three separate books made a point of saying that Carolyn Hayward never got married," I said, sitting down. "They could have included something else instead."

"Of course. God forbid a woman not get married," Sairah said. "Did they mention anything about kids?"

"All the books I read today stated she never had kids," I said.

"Typical," Sairah scoffed. "We have one job, right?"

"I don't get it," Faiz said. "Shouldn't they include that? It is relevant. The Hayward line died with her."

"It's so frustrating," I said. "I'm tired of reading a list of remarkable things this woman did and then it ends with, 'But she never got married or had kids.' What does that have to do with anything? You could do everything – literally save lives – and then you're a disappointment because you didn't get married or start a family. These are outdated ideas about who we're supposed to be and what we're supposed to do." Goalposts in a game we didn't sign up for or know we were playing.

"And we're still talking about them," Sairah said. "It was one thing when Carolyn was alive, but we still have to deal with this. Laan, when were those books written?"

"I wrote it down," I said. "1981, 1988 and 2003. So not that long ago."

* * *

As a child, five minutes felt like an eternity. I remember realising time had started passing quicker as I got older when someone pointed it out to me. There's a word for this, I think, but I can't remember.

Nobody told me time would collapse like an accordion. Nobody told me about those moments when you hear a sound that pierces through the years, reaches out and yanks you back to when you were eleven and you first heard that song on the radio. Or you see a bike and you feel shaken and suddenly you're five and that's your bike and you just fell off it and scraped your knee.

Or sometimes you don't know what it reminds you of, or you don't know what the cue is. You just feel a sense of dread, or regret, or longing deep in your stomach and you have to carry that with you as you move throughout the day, not sure where you went wrong.

* * *

"Have you heard The Kicks' new album?" Sairah asked.

"Oh yeah, I liked that song 'Wrench'," I said, pulling out my phone. "See, I put it on my funeral playlist."

"You have a funeral playlist?" Faiz said.

"You don't?" I replied. "Most important function of your life and you're going to leave the music up to chance? I could never."

"She's just excited," Sairah said.

"You're excited... to die?" Faiz asked.

"Not to die," I said. "Or at least, it's not like I want to die. I kind of feel neutral about it. I like living, and I'll definitely miss it, and there are so many things I'd feel sad about dying without doing. But at the same time there are things I'm looking forward to about death. Like getting all the answers. And having a cool funeral."

"You won't even be able to go to it," Faiz said.

"If she was a ghost then…" Sairah said.

"Who knows? Maybe I'll be able to watch from somewhere. Maybe I'll just know what happened. Maybe I won't. Takes off some of the pressure. Another answer."

"How can you be so nonchalant about it?" he asked.

"It's going to happen. There's no point being sad about it," I said with a shrug, then added, "I have to admit I am kind of sad I won't be able to go to my funeral after putting so much effort into it."

"Then why do it?" Faiz said.

"Dying is, in a way, like moving on to the next stage of your life, like being born, or going to college. So, a funeral is like a going away or graduation party. My graduation party was a disaster, and I learned my lesson. So, this is why I take a lot of care in the details of one of the most important events in my life. Hopefully I still have plenty of time to prepare."

I could see Faiz trying to understand what I said. "So… do you have your wedding playlist planned out too?"

"Whoa, who said anything about a wedding?" I laughed.

"Because we're *girls* we should be planning our *weddings*?" Sairah said.

"That's not happening anytime soon," I said. "Or maybe never."

"See, Laana's right," Sairah said.

"I always am," I interjected.

"Everyone dies," Sairah said. "Not everyone gets married. So, it makes more sense to plan for your funeral than your wedding. Also, who wants to plan a wedding?"

"Sounds stressful. I don't like that we're supposed to all be planning something we may not end up doing, but there's this thing we're all going to go through that we can't talk about, that we know nothing about, that we're supposed to pretend doesn't exist," I said.

"Laana, it terrifies me," Faiz said. "I've never been so scared. For that reason: that we don't know anything about it, and there's no way of knowing."

"Well, if you make a funeral playlist, at least you'll know what music they'll play," Sairah said.

"You have another graduation coming up," Faiz pointed out. "Aren't you going to plan that first?"

"Oh that," I said, waving the idea away.

"Another thing that may not happen," Sairah said.

"Who knows if I'll finish at this rate," I said.

"Maybe if you did your actual research instead of chasing some made-up ghost…" he said.

"Um, she was very much real, thank you," I said.

"Unlike Laana's PhD, which is hypothetical at this point," Sairah said.

"Research is about getting sucked into rabbit holes," I said.

"No, it's not," Faiz said.

"I don't think so," Sairah laughed.

"I don't see either of you doing any research," I said.

"Yeah, that's your thing," Faiz said.

"It's because it's so difficult," Sairah said, reaching out to pat my hand. "You're the only one cut out for it."

"Or the only one stubborn enough to commit to it," Faiz said.

"I don't think it's stubbornness," I said.

"You have to be stubborn to think you're going to get to the bottom of something like this," he said.

★ ★ ★

In the book in my hand, there is a sketch of Hayward Manor looking like an illustration from the classic novels we read as kids. This book described how the Haywards built their house.

It's weird that there was a time when it didn't exist, and neither did my house or any of my friends' houses, even Devon's ancient house that's been renovated who knows how many times. And then somehow it grew, tall and imposing, and then a wall grew and then vines grew to the point that most of it was obscured. It was so huge, yet I'd seen so little of it.

I can't really focus on the house's history. Instead, I start thinking about what it's like holding life in your hands, how Carolyn must have felt. I wondered if she'd ever had to give a vaccine, knowing that with that sharp burst of pain she was preventing much greater suffering. I wondered what she wondered about.

I wonder what it would have been like to lose your parents right before you lost your own life. How fast did news travel back then and how long did it take to get back to her? How hard and long did she grieve before she became the person others grieved? Who grieved her? How much did she remember before being remembered? How many memories did she play over and over again in her mind, how many times did she rewrite their stories, how many things did she regret? How much did she speculate, who did she confide in, how much did she show, how much did she allow herself to feel? How did she mourn?

Maybe she threw herself into her work. Maybe she withdrew further inside her home, inside herself. Did she experience all the emotions, or just one: overwhelming guilt?

How did she grieve? And was it the right way, the noble way? Was she responsible and respectful and respectable?

All of these gaps, and no way to address them.

★ ★ ★

I went back to the library for another round of books on Carolyn, returning the dead ends. One of the books from Faiz's book report – *Local Legends of Connecticut* – was in the children's section. As I approached the shelves, fragments returned to me of myself at age four or five dragging books practically half my size across the carpet, building a stack of books on the ground and plopping down next to it. I saw my mom in between the bookcases, sitting on the floor with her back to the wall. Her hair was longer than it is now. She pointed out details in the illustrations to me while we read. I was too impatient and kept interrupting her.

I pulled *Local Legends of Connecticut* off the shelf. There were brightly coloured, smiling cartoon figures of historical people on the cover. I wonder how they would feel about their depictions. If it would hurt more or less than an epitaph you didn't like on your gravestone, or an incorrect line in your biography.

I turned to the chapter called "Nurse Carolyn".

> *Carolyn Hayward worked at Clifton Children's Hospital. Her parents built it to take care of the kids in the neighbourhood. She was smart, worked hard at school and studied to become a nurse because she wanted to take care of people. She decided to work in the hospital her parents built because she loved kids and helping her community.*

There was no mention of her death.

★ ★ ★

Mom wanted me to sort through some of my shelves. I think she mainly wanted me to get rid of my stuff. I don't blame her; I have a lot of things. And they just sit here, untouched. Amara used to tease me for being so old-fashioned and only buying things in hard copies – books, magazines, records, CDs, cassette tapes – outdated physical forms. And I kept it all. I don't know what for – memories? A record? Proof? Research? Who knows?

For my thirteenth birthday, Faiz gave me a book of butterfly moments in history. The writer who sold the copyright to what became her most famous book. The actress who passed up a role for a movie that turned out to be a runaway box office hit.

Moments like that, surprises, turning points, things that could have been different but for one thing, unexplained connections, decisions that changed lives. I put it in the keep pile to read later.

★ ★ ★

"It's so... strange to think about where everyone ended up," I said.

"Yeah, I always wonder how they reached that decision – if they changed or they were like that all along, that there was some side to them you missed," Sairah said, looking up from her notebook.

"I never thought Faiz would have stayed here," I said. "I really thought he just wanted to leave."

"I didn't think I would still be here," Sairah said.

"Yeah, you were supposed to be successful and famous," I said.

"And instead I'm stuck."

"Well, I didn't really know what I was doing, and still don't. Maybe we switched? Some cosmic mix-up?"

Sairah laughed.

"Weird you and Faiz don't hang out, though," I said. "Could have bonded over your thwarted escape plans."

"I just don't think we ever really got along," she said.

"Every time I log onto Facebook or Instagram or even Twitter, someone's getting engaged or accepted into law school or finding a new job," I said.

"I know, it sucks," she said. "I thought we had at least a few years until this would start."

"We've all been alive for the same amount of time, but we're at completely different places. Except it's annoying because it feels like everyone's moving forward somehow."

"When will it end?"

"30s, 40s, 50s?"

"No, because then you have second marriages and kids' report cards and then they get into college and get married and start having their own kids."

"Did you ever feel that when you were younger you had all these possibilities, just endless opportunities," I asked, leaning over my coffee. "When you're really young, it feels like you could be whatever you wanted. Then you realise you have certain skills, and you take certain classes and all of a sudden you have a major and then work experience in a specific field and it's too late to change. You have these moments where time and possibility splinter, but you don't see the threads. All you see is the one reality you're locked into."

"I've wanted to be a writer for as long as I can remember. That's all I ever wanted to be – except for that year in high school I wanted to be a psychologist."

"So, you could have just as easily become a therapist."

"Not really. I only became one of those things. Looking back, it seems like only some outcomes were inevitable. The rest of the time, it's just infinite possibilities."

"It feels as though some things were random or sudden, until I look back and see that there were threads all the time. It's like everything's some indication of the future."

"And at the time, you can't figure out what any of it means."

★ ★ ★

I wrote down all my notes about Carolyn in old brown leather notebooks. It felt right. Taking notes on my phone in shorthand was somehow incorrect. Like falling out of time, getting lost in the sequence. A relic in the wrong section of a museum, the wrong era, they got the label wrong.

I filled out the last of a set of notebooks Daadi gave me when I started university. I asked Dad and he gave me one of his he'd only half-used. Now I was running out of pages again. I asked for extras. There were none.

I went to one of the three bookstores in the centre of town. One was a big chain, one was a tiny second-hand bookstore, and one was a slightly higher-end independent shop which sold fancy writing equipment and had a good café. It was, at one point, Sairah's favourite place to hang out. She bought all of her Moleskines there, even some calligraphy equipment during a phase. She would haul a stack of poetry books and lay them on a café table as we worked, taking breaks to scribble in her Moleskine.

I shouldn't have been surprised by the changes to the layout. The café was downstairs. Writing equipment was upstairs. The black walls had been painted over in deep blues and reds. I navigated my way towards the notebooks. I was browsing the leather diaries when I remembered the unique colours Sairah would find for hers: lime green, lavender, peach.

I saw a flash of hair out of the corner of my eye and, for a split second, I thought I conjured her. An apparition triggered by memories, which laughed with Sairah's loud, abrupt giggle.

Except it actually was her, with two other women our age who I didn't recognise. They didn't know who I was either. They looked straight through me as I scanned their faces searching for a clue, any hint of where I might have seen them before, or who they were. Sairah saw me and yelled, "Laana! Hey guys, this is Laana, my best friend since, well," she laughed. "Since forever!"

I exchanged smiles with the two of them and shook hands, as Sairah made introductions. I racked my brain for any mention of their names. Nothing came up. Sairah had mentioned she had new friends – had I just not bothered to remember them?

★ ★ ★

Faiz had a peanut allergy and always carried an EpiPen with him. We knew this from countless birthday parties, school lunches and bake sales. Sometimes he'd forget it, which always shocked me. I thought you would remember something that vital, but when it's always there I guess it starts to feel less important.

I often wondered if it was a conscious choice to remember it, to bring it. Or was it a habit? Was it like grabbing a jacket just in case it got cold, or like putting on shoes before leaving the house? Each time he picked it up, did he know, did he realise, did he think about the power it had to save his life? Did he feel like he was holding his own life in his hands? Was he choosing life, was he thinking about self-preservation, or is self-preservation just a series of habits and routines?

★ ★ ★

"So, I was in the cemetery –" I began.

"Hi Laana, how are you?" Faiz interjected. "Hi Faiz, how are you?"

I rolled my eyes. "And I saw Carolyn."

"Your real friend," Faiz said.

"As I was saying, I was walking through the cemetery, like I do every day."

"You go to the cemetery every day?"

"You know people used to hang out in cemeteries for fun? It was like going to the park."

"We have a park."

I waved him away. "Yeah, but it's boring."

"Also, too many bad memories," Sairah said.

"Too many bad memories at the park, but not the cemetery?" Faiz asked, incredulous.

"We're not the ones who died," Sairah said. "But I did lose things at the park."

"I have really nice memories of the cemetery," I said. "It's funny, my mom used to spend a lot of time there when she was younger. It's almost like –"

"A family thing?" Sairah asked. I nodded.

"I saw Carolyn's grave," I said. "And it's so weird to think that there's an actual person in there. Well, not a person, exactly."

Faiz winced.

"But you know, what's left of a body at this point," I said.

"A physical counterpart to the ghost," Sairah said.

"It's weird, isn't it?" I said. "The ghost feels so real and vivid, we forget something physical was definitely left behind. But it's almost easier to accept the ghost."

"You want to exhume the body," Faiz said slowly. "So, you can perform an autopsy?"

I sighed. "Unbelievable."

"Don't be ridiculous," Sairah said. "We're going to resurrect her and ask her what happened."

Faiz looked at her, wary. I laughed.

"Don't worry, I'm not actually a witch," Sairah said.

"It would have been useful," I said.

★ ★ ★

Time isn't necessarily linear, at least not the way you experience it. It's not flat, it's not happening all at once. It's more of an accordion. Sometimes it's all stretched out, and you can't remember the plot of that movie you saw last Friday, or that you had a hair appointment scheduled for next week. You can't remember what you wore two days ago or how long it's been since you last went to the dentist. But sometimes it's scrunched up, the days, weeks, months, and years folding in on each other, certain words or phrases or smells or feelings or sounds or images echoing through time, bouncing around inside your head. Sometimes something reaches through time, through all the layers, and sucks you back with it, and you don't even know what year it is anymore.

The details start to blur, and you don't remember anything.

Chapter 4

City Hall has one room that serves as a miniscule museum. I didn't even know why we had a museum, but I hoped it might suddenly prove useful. The room was about half the size of my parents' living room. One wall was covered by an illustrated timeline of the town's history with labels and explanations in mismatched fonts. In a space carved out of the wall, behind a glass panel, was the city's charter. There was an early map on the other side of the room. Four photographs adorned the wall in between, plastered onto the surface, enlarged to the point they were pixelated.

No sign of Carolyn or her diary. No mention of the Haywards.

I went to the back of the building where the archives were.

"Hi, I'm looking for Carolyn Hayward's diary," I said to the receptionist.

"Can I ask why?" she responded.

"Research project," I said, delivered more like a question than an answer.

"Can I see some ID?"

I handed over my driver's license. Turns out it's super useful in Clifton. Not so much in the city.

She went out into the stacks. I followed her. She pressed a button on the side of the motorised bookcase and they moved, compressing the shelves to create an opening. She went in, and for a split second I was worried the shelves would move again and swallow her whole, crushing her into nothingness. She emerged holding a box. Then she tilted her head sideways, signalling me to follow her.

We walked to the reading room, where she laid two pieces of foam on the table. She took the cover off the box, then removed the plastic sheet that wrapped the book. She placed the slim, brown leather notebook onto the foam and opened it.

I leaned over. The first few pages had faded to the point that the writing was faint, and you wouldn't be able to tell anyone had used it if it weren't for the uneven light bronze tint. The archivist turned the pages. They started to show signs of writing. Scribbles here and there, but nothing intelligible. Slowly the words began to float up and become visible. It was hard to make out Carolyn's writing.

"You know how everyone always jokes about doctors having terrible handwriting?" I asked.

The receptionist paused, but didn't look up or laugh. She kept turning the pages. I could read a sentence and, below it, another one:

> *It still feels like they're here with me... Sometimes I swear I can hear Mother's voice calling me from the dining room... I see a shadow and turn, expecting Father to be there, but no one is.*

We kept turning. Two pages later:

> *The hospital is getting crowded. Some doctors say we should stop admitting any more patients. I think we need to expand. There should be more space for children and infants.*

The receptionist turned another page.

★ ★ ★

While grocery shopping, an old song came on. I remembered hearing it for the first time years ago, on the radio in the car with my parents.

Dad turned it up, saying he used to love it. "You can't really get away with liking it now," he said. "Everyone says it hasn't aged well."

"I hate when people say something hasn't aged well," Mom said. "Time isn't the problem. It was wrong from the beginning."

I can't help but think how different I am from my parents just because I was born later. All the slang I know, how much easier technology is for me, how my views are different. And then I think about my hypothetical kids, and their hypothetical kids. What technology they'll know how to use that I won't, views they'll have that will shock me, what they'll listen to and watch and read. What beliefs will become outdated. What they'll think is cool or progressive. What they'll make of what I did with my life. What they'll think of me. I want to see where things go from here, knowing I won't fully understand. Knowing it won't be for me, and I won't be able to keep up, and that I'll be the backwards one. Knowing I'll fall behind.

★ ★ ★

"What are you doing, stalking Carolyn online?" Faiz asked. "It's not like she has social media or anything."

"Imagine if she did, though," I said. "It would make this so much easier. Think of how much we're going to leave behind."

"Ugh, I don't want to," Faiz said.

"We have so much of a record," Sairah said. "Carolyn had almost nothing. A two-year-old has days' worth of footage of them already."

"All that information and it still isn't the full picture," I said.

"It's all curated," Sairah said.

"I'm always honest," Faiz said.

"I always feel like I'm playing a part," I said. "I post things because I feel like I should. Because other people posted something similar." I'm not lying or hiding anything, but I can't show people who I am fully. I feel like I'm showing them different versions of myself.

"Like you're playing you," Sairah said.

"But is it really me?" I replied.

"I can't answer that," Sairah said. "All I get is a version too."

"This conversation is making my brain hurt," Faiz said.

I sipped my coffee. At once all three of our phones, sitting face up on the café table, lit up. The white bubbles told us a famous singer had died.

"A lot of obituaries are written ahead of time," Sairah said.

"That can't be right," I said.

"How else would they be able to get all this up within minutes?" Sairah said, turning the phone to face me and flicking her finger, scrolling through paragraphs.

"So, someone is predicting or guessing deaths?" I asked.

"And someone else is writing about the living as if they are already dead," she said.

"Dark," said Faiz. "Can we switch topics?"

I ignored him and turned to Sairah. "I guess I should start working on a draft."

Sairah nodded, looking relieved. "I can't leave it up to chance. Everyone else would get something wrong. You're okay with doing it, right?"

"Yeah. It's not like it's an authorised biography or anything" I said. Sairah put down her cup, eyebrows raised. "Don't get any ideas," I said.

★ ★ ★

From *A History of South-Eastern Connecticut*, page 193:

> *Clifton Hospital became the state's first hospital dedicated entirely to children in 1859. It was initially called Hayward Hospital, after the people who founded it, Charles and Annabelle Hayward. Their daughter, Carolyn, worked there and established the hospital's children's wing. All three of them died in a fire at their home, Hayward Manor, now a historic landmark.*

★ ★ ★

Taylor's dad and my dad were friends. My dad used to take me to the record store with him when I was younger, while he looked for some rare LP he badly wanted. He would exchange recommendations with Taylor's dad, who had a similar taste in music. Taylor was four years older than me and had graduated high school before I even started, but we became good friends when I was six and she was ten. While our dads talked about things that didn't interest us, we would reorganise the displays and rearrange the rows of CDs and crates of vinyl, keeping an ear out for whatever our fathers were talking about, and then making sure they couldn't find it. As we got older, we exchanged CDs and recommendations, as our music tastes became similar and then diverged. She convinced her dad to stock the metal magazine I was reading at the time. I worked at the record store during the summers in high school, mostly just stacking records and labelling shelves – this time putting things where they *should* be. Taylor's dad retired a few years ago and let Taylor take over. She had reorganised the shop. I went straight for the second-hand records which now lined the back walls. They used to be in crates in a side room, which made them less visible and less exciting for people browsing the shop. But Taylor was the biggest advocate for buying second-hand.

"I don't want those," I said, thirteen years old. "They're somebody else's hand-me-downs."

"You check books out from the library," she said.

"But that's different. I give them back later. I don't hold onto them and read them over and over."

"Music doesn't just belong to you; it belongs to everybody."

"But why would I buy an old one when I could buy a new one?"

"It's cheaper?"

"Okay, I'm interested."

"Think about it like you're giving it a second life. Nothing lives just one life. Think of all the things you pass around, all the different people you've been."

"I don't want to think about the other mes," I groaned.

* * *

"I'm glad you're doing all this research on Carolyn," Sairah said. I turned to look at her. "I'm very concerned for you, but happy for me."

"I've learned so much about her," I said. "I'd always heard about her and knew nothing."

"She could have done anything, and that includes nothing. But she didn't. Instead, she put her time and effort into helping people."

"Do you ever wonder how many women have stories like that? Like they did so much, and nobody notices?"

"Oh, before I forget." Sairah passed me a piece of paper. It was a little faded, but barely creased or wrinkled. I looked at it and then at her, before opening it up. I recognised my old handwriting. "You just had this lying around?"

"You made me promise to keep it safe, remember?" she said. "You made me swear on a stack of notebooks. You said I would be in charge of your funeral if I hadn't died before you. I mean, it's a pretty big responsibility for anyone, let alone a twelve-year-old, especially with your list of demands."

I had spent hours thinking it through and deliberating where I would be buried (the local cemetery, next to the pond preferably), what they would do with my body (straight into the ground, no coffin, no gravestone) and my funeral.

The funeral was the tricky part. There were too many options. I couldn't decide who would be invited (did I want a big or small funeral?), what kind of music (did I want a sad, sombre gathering, or a fun party? In the end I settled for sad, but gradually more upbeat) and what other demands I could make (how did I want to be remembered?). Do I give everyone time to grieve? Do I give them something to remember me by? Do I ask them to be happy, to celebrate what I've done? Aren't funerals for the living, anyway? Isn't death for the living too?

But then there were even more questions I couldn't answer. How was I going to die? Painlessly, I hope. Is it just abrupt nothingness, and the next thing you know you're at the next stage, perfectly conscious like when you wake up after hours of sleep and you think you just lay down seconds ago? Or is it a different kind of sleep? Are you meant to wait in darkness for a while? Are you conscious of the darkness? Do you feel yourself wait? Do you dream while you wait?

I read through the detailed list, each paragraph in a different colour of gel pen. "Yeah, this is pretty much the same as what my plans are now."

"Would you want to know when you were going to die?" Sairah asked.

I considered the question.

"I would," she answered herself. "If I knew how long I had to live, I'd abandon everything and focus on one book so I could finish it. That way I wouldn't have to worry about people publishing an unfinished version after I die."

"So, you could publish it on your own terms." I was still thinking about my answer. There's nothing I want to do that I could accomplish in any amount of time. "I think I'd want to be surprised," I said finally. "I guess that takes the pressure off."

★ ★ ★

My parents are professors. My mom currently teaches engineering, my dad teaches math. My mom has flipped back and forth between different levels of education – elementary school, high school, college – while my dad has stayed pretty consistently a university professor.

My parents didn't really care about whether I was good at math or not. They just wanted to share their enthusiasm and excitement about learning in general, which I guess I retained or, rather, inherited. From all the counting songs my mom used to sing in the car with me on the way to school to watching my parents sitting on opposite sides of the dining table animatedly talking through my algebra textbook, exclaiming terminology in unison as they tried to solve my homework problems with me. For them, it was a fun activity more than the devastatingly boring task I thought it was.

I wasn't great at math – I was decent at it until I became subpar, but thanks to my parents I always liked it. They framed math problems as a mystery. You had to decode, decrypt, unearth the answers. An equation was like a sentence, and you just had to translate, synthesise, rearrange, and summarise until you distilled it down to its core truth.

"Why do I have to do math if it's so hard?" I remember nine-year-old me pouting at the dinner table.

"Because you can't learn if you're always doing things you already know how to do," Mom replied from the other room.

"You shouldn't be scared of hard things," Dad said. "You should try."

"But… it's so frustrating," I whined.

"I know," Dad said. "But the difficult things can be the best for you. They're often the right thing, sometimes the enjoyable thing, a lot of times the thing that's good for you. It's the difficult things that help you grow and learn."

"I'm not learning anything," I said. "I can't even figure out the answer."

"Sometimes it takes a while," Dad said. "Don't turn your back on something just because you didn't succeed the first couple of times."

"How many times is it going to take?"

"I don't know. But you can't give up. There's an answer in there somewhere."

★ ★ ★

"What exactly are we looking for?" Sairah asked, as she sifted through her pile of old newspaper clippings. Faiz pulled a stack out of a box.

"Any references to the Haywards, their house, hospital, or a fire," I said.

"I mean, we're just going to end up with a big pile," Faiz said. "Anytime someone gets injured, they get sent straight to the one hospital."

"Should we be looking for malaria or influenza?" Sairah asked. "Or any other diseases or outbreaks?"

"Or ghost sightings?" Faiz asked.

I squinted at the tiny faded print on the narrow clipping in my hand, preserved in a plastic sheet. It was a single column wide. The clipping was yellow, faded more in certain spots than others. The rounded parts of letters stuck out at me sharply, stinging my eyes, frustrating me by generating possibilities for what the word might say. I couldn't make out the sentences. The edges and ends danced before me.

"I don't know," I said. "Just look for anything that might look like it's connected to Carolyn."

I picked up another clipping. The story was about Carolyn's parents' death. Nothing new. The text matched up with most of what I'd been reading.

"Did you ever realise the word fatal has fate in it?" I asked.

Sairah frowned and shook her head, not shifting her eyes from the clipping she was holding.

"I got a fire!" Faiz said. "Hayward Hospital – oh wait – this is after Carolyn died."

"Still useful," I said.

"Why are we even looking at records that came after Carolyn?" he asked. Sairah and I shrugged without looking at each other.

We sorted through the boxes in silence for a few moments. I saw an image of the building that became our high school. It was, as far as I could tell, always a school. But it was smaller back then. They just kept adding to it. The article was about the first addition. I paused and looked up. "Hey, do you remember 'The War of the Ghosts'?"

Sairah looked up and stared off over my shoulder. "You know, I remember it was a memory experiment, but I can't remember anything else about it."

'The War of the Ghosts' is a psychology experiment, named after the indigenous folk story used in the study. My high school psychology teacher tried it out on us. On Monday, he told us a story. On Wednesday, he had us write down what we remembered.

The theory is that your brain remembers the narrative in a way that makes sense to you and maps it onto the structures you're used to using, stories you're used to hearing. Basically, you remember it in a way that matches up to how you see the world. You tend to forget any non-essential details. You also forget anything that feels unfamiliar to you.

"I'm surprised so many people in our class didn't remember the ghosts," I said. "Like, wouldn't you have remembered it as being a ghost story? Wouldn't you have thought, 'This is a ghost story'. Wouldn't you think, 'Oh, today I walked into psych class and Mr. B told us a ghost story'?"

"It wasn't Mr. B," Faiz said. "We had him senior year. Junior year we had Doyle."

"Whatever, you know what I mean. Wouldn't you just be so struck by the ghosts that you remembered them? Like, don't people remember what stood out?"

"It's hard to remember when you don't really care," Sairah said.

"You know, I was so confused by the plot of the story I couldn't tell you what happened ten seconds after hearing it," Faiz said. "It didn't make any sense to me."

"You sure it was Doyle?" I asked. "I could have sworn it was Mr. B."

★ ★ ★

I remember hearing about confirmation bias for the first time and immediately wanting to discount it – ironic, in hindsight. But I just couldn't accept it, because if it was true that would mean it was hard to learn anything new. What's the point of learning at all then? What's the point of doing, seeing, experiencing anything new if you're only going to process it based on something you already know? Can you really have any new experiences if you're only interpreting them as fitting the mould of a past belief? We tend to prefer familiarity. How do we ever break out?

Trends are cyclical. Are we just trapped in concentric circles, little rings, paddocks, keeping us perpetually retreading the same paths, doomed to repeat the same mistakes?

★ ★ ★

"What's that?" Sairah asked, as I flipped through the notes I took at City Hall.

"Notes from Carolyn's journal," I responded, gaze down in the book. Sairah didn't say anything, so I looked at her briefly.

"You think it's too intrusive?" I asked.

She shrugged. "I feel like speculating about anyone is sort of intrusive."

"But that's everything I've been doing."

"Imagining people not as they are feels… weird," she said.

"Do you think it's disrespectful to look into Carolyn's life like this?"

"You're just reading history books."

"Oh, you'd be surprised what people have got away with putting in history textbooks. And leaving out."

"Good point. But still. It's not like you're reading her texts."

"What would her equivalent of texts have been?"

"Letters?"

"They always publish those, and journals."

"That's why I'm already three steps ahead. No one's getting their hands on my stuff." She held up the notebook she had been writing in.

"Thanks to me."

"Thanks to you. What would I do without you?"

★ ★ ★

My mom once got me a book from the library about women who made important contributions to science, and I read it and reread it and kept checking it out so much the librarians told me I had to give it a break. I liked how some of the stories were really funny – things were invented haphazardly, discovered by accident, or occurred by chance. At the time, I hadn't given much thought as to who had invented or found them, or even that they had been created or discovered at all. They were just there.

But there were so many entries. So many others that had taken time and years. Women who had worked their whole lives – in some cases forgotten or overlooked or erased. The way I had heard people talk about science, even at that age, had told me that there were few women in it. But reading the book from cover to cover, I knew that wasn't true.

My mother always encouraged me to be interested in science, but I never really enjoyed it. She used to do research before she started teaching.

I'd notice her excitement when they released engineering toys for little girls. I'd seen how encouraging she was when Amara's older sister said she was going to engineering school. She judged the science fair at school one year – one of the only times a woman had been invited to judge. In the years after, they made sure to include women on the panel every time.

★ ★ ★

Sairah called to tell me about a true crime podcast she started listening to. "It's on how the people in this town disappeared or died mysteriously," she says. "Hey, do you remember that movie we watched when you slept over in the fourth grade? About the ghost hunters?"

"I'm drawing a blank. I can't remember anything that happened in fourth grade."

"I'm sure nothing worth remembering happened in fourth grade. Anyway, that's where they were hunting for ghosts. Obviously, the story in the movie is completely different from how it happened in real life."

"People love embellishing."

"I'd say it's forgivable most of the time."

"Is that how Ms. Durrani felt about your history exam?"

"That wasn't embellishing. That was just plain old forgetting. Which, if you think about it, is really at the essence of history. So, I was just making a big statement about the very nature of the discipline."

"Wrong discipline, Sairah," I said. "You were always good at coming up with stories – the fictional kind, at least."

* * *

"*Wuthering Heights* was a ghost story," Sairah said.

"No it wasn't," I said. "I don't remember any ghosts."

"There are ghosts, but it's not clear whether they're imagined or not," she said.

"So, it's not a ghost story," I said.

"It is."

"How can it be a ghost story if you don't know if the ghosts are real or not?"

"Because you don't know they're not real."

"So, you don't know if it's a ghost story."

"It's not not a ghost story."

I groaned. "In the event I do die before you do, I am definitely coming back to haunt you."

"You don't even believe in ghosts."

"Just because I don't believe in them now doesn't mean they don't exist."

"So, you don't know if they're real or not."

"They're not not real. You can't rule anything out."

Faiz slid into the booth. "More ghost talk?" he said.

"I'm sorry, how was work?" I said with a fake polite smile.

"Ugh, don't ask," he said by way of reply.

"Okay, back to ghosts —" I tried to get in quickly and unsuccessfully.

"I hate my job, I hate living here, I wish I could just sit around all day and do whatever you two do," he said.

"Work," Sairah said. "That's what we do, same as you."

"Well, you seem to enjoy it a lot more," he said.

"Not as much as you'd think," Sairah said. "It's a struggle for everyone, not just you. It's a phase of life thing. We're all going through it."

"How long is this phase supposed to last?" Faiz asked.

"I read that quarter-life crises happen in early adulthood, and can happen — this is from an article — as early as eighteen and go on as late as forty," I said.

Sairah gaped at me. "I have potentially fifteen more years of this?"

"Forty is early adulthood?" Faiz asked. "How long do these people expect to live?"

"You're not having quarter-life crises," I said, moving my head between the both of them.

"I can't succeed at the one thing I want to do and I live at home," Sairah said.

"I live at home and I hate my job," Faiz said.

"Isn't that normal?" I asked. "Doesn't everyone have things they want to change?"

"You don't," Sairah said.

"I think I'm having a different crisis," I said.

★ ★ ★

Sometimes you think about things you wish you hadn't said. Or things you wish you did. Or things you could have done had you not overslept and then, in your hurry, knocked a cup of coffee onto your laptop and lost all your work. Or what would have happened had you not missed the bus because you ran into an old friend and started talking. Or how things would be now had you not cancelled your trip home a month ago at the last minute.

Sometimes you think about how things could be different – almost completely, entirely different – if you had done one tiny thing differently. Not overslept, not missed the bus, picked up a phone call, gone home for the weekend, decided to send in an application for a job you thought you weren't good enough for. Sometimes you can trace a lot of things you don't like about life back to that moment. Sometimes it's bigger moments: a move, a friend, a job, which college, which major, a family member. You think about all the moments you spent with people, and how many more you could have had.

And you think about all the things you have because of these split-second decisions, or things that happened suddenly, out of your control, seemingly randomly. And it gets hard to think about things like fate and paths and options. It's hard to wonder if you're really meant to be where you are when you don't like where you are. You want to take back all those bad moments and replace them with good ones. Or just replace them with moments. You want more time, different outcomes, but you can't predict the consequences. You want to change one thing, but you don't know if those ripples were actually meant to be waves under different conditions. The butterfly effect versus regret.

★ ★ ★

We're not supposed to think about death or talk about it. It's one of the only universal human experiences – next to being born – but we know so little about it and we barely ever discuss it. I thought I was just interested in it because I'd been lucky enough to be spared loss or mourning or grief. And I thought once I did lose someone, I'd feel differently. I'd no longer want to visit cemeteries or read ghost stories. That it would be painful. But it didn't really change. I still wanted to do research on it, to talk about it, to plan my funeral, to look up burial methods, and listen to songs about cemeteries.

★ ★ ★

I was walking to the cemetery for another jog, when I saw a figure in the distance, standing in front of the gates. For a split second I didn't recognise who it was and felt my breath catch. Could it be her, finally, in the place she was buried? But I went closer, saw Sairah and was doubly disappointed to not have instantly been able to tell it was her.

"I guessed this was where you'd be." She shrugged and leaned against one of the pillars by the gate. "You're so predictable."

"You hate predictability," I said.

"In myself, yes," she said. "In other people, it's comforting."

We started walking, not really knowing where we were going, and not thinking to ask the other. Soon, we ended up in front of Hayward Manor. Sairah stopped. "Wait, this is where you were bringing me?"

"I thought you were taking me somewhere."

"No, I was following you."

"Well, it's not like I had a destination in mind."

"Then it was subconscious."

I shot her a look, then something on the wall caught my eye. It was a new addition to the collage of notices signalling the long-awaited demolition of Hayward Manor.

"Funny they would put up another notice," I said. "When

they were supposed to destroy this house years ago."

"Clifton's always been like that," Sairah said. "It's always almost about to change, and then years go by and everything's the same. It's stuck in between, keeps trying to move, and then we keep getting pulled back to the way things always were. It's like time's frozen."

"It's not exactly frozen," I said. "I mean we're here."

"Our parents moved here a few decades ago," Sairah said. "That was the last big change that happened."

"Things change all the time."

"Little things change. Shops close and open, houses are rebuilt, but nothing major. You're an architect. How old are all of our buildings?"

"Failed architect."

"Okay, so expert in old things."

"Accurate, but not exactly fair. Our houses are older than us and even our parents."

"All the big landmarks in this town are old buildings – the Manor, the hospital, City Hall, the park is ancient. Not to mention the cemetery, which is oddly huge for a town of this size."

I didn't realise that until she pointed it out. "It's so much history and death."

"Maybe Carolyn cursed us."

"She was probably just trying to protect the town."

"Ghost apologist," Sairah muttered.

"Do you think they'll ever destroy Hayward Manor?" I asked after a while.

Sairah shrugged. "I mean, it's a house that no one lives in and no one can even go into. It's not really serving a purpose, and I don't see what purpose it could have."

"Not to mention everything everyone knows about it is probably fake."

"I'm sure destroying her house isn't gonna stop Carolyn from her haunting – sorry, protecting. In fact, it might make her angry or more determined."

"She doesn't need her house anymore. And nobody's worried about her anger or feelings. If they were, they wouldn't tell those stories about her."

We walked over the hill to the edge of the cemetery. "How many notebooks are you at now?" I asked.

"How many?"

"Yeah, just gotta make sure I'm stocked up on lighter fluid."

She laughed. "About eleven... and three hard drives." She looked at me.

"I'll make sure to buy an axe or a mallet or whatever you use to crush hard drives."

"Do whatever you have to. My life's work will be in your hands. I trust you to do what it takes."

"I don't know if I want to leave a trace. But you've always known."

"I want my trace to be bigger, to make more of an impact than I do."

"I just can't stand parts of me out there without... me."

"Which is why you're gonna burn all my stuff."

"What if you don't finish? I mean, obviously, hopefully, probably not, but do you ever worry, like, what if you don't finish?"

"I'd rather have nothing out there than something I wasn't ready to share. Something incomplete." After a pause, she said. "It's easy to see how death became an aesthetic."

I looked at her, eyebrows raised. "It's an aesthetic?"

"Yeah, like Gothic literature... and other stuff."

"I don't know, I never thought of that aesthetic as being based on death. Fear, maybe. Darkness, things you're not supposed to talk about. I guess that all applies to death. But I don't think death can be an aesthetic. That's like saying loss is an aesthetic."

"I guess... but cemeteries are a part of that."

"That's not really death. It's more memorialisation? I guess that's the aestheticisation of history," I said, then walked past three graves. "I don't know. It seems weird, almost disrespectful, to turn death into an aesthetic."

"I guess maybe it's the idea of death, or the taboo surrounding it."

"But I think it's impossible to collapse all of it, the loss, the memory, the grief, even just non-emotional thinking about death into an aesthetic. Or to flatten or detach one part from the others. I don't think you can disentangle any of it."

"But what about people who visit cemeteries, like tourists? All the famous cemeteries."

"I get that that happens. I go to this cemetery all the time. But I'm not doing it for how it looks. It's what it reminds me of, weirdly my mom and my friends. And what it makes me feel: less scared and less worried about what will happen. And those people are probably just going to see some piece of history, what used to be there."

"Maybe it's a little bit like horror: take fear and turn it into entertainment."

"I think that's true, but I think some of it is deeper. Confront your fear? Interrogate it? Figure out what's scary and what isn't?"

"I wonder if taking death and using it to inspire whatever you want to call it. I wonder if that was someone's way of coping with it."

★ ★ ★

I felt like I met a different version of Carolyn each day. But then there were different versions of me, too. There are so many versions of me in people's heads, online, in my own plans and hopes and dreams. I could pick a different one each day, put it on and take it off like a jacket, throw it on the back of a chair when I'm done or leave it on the bus or bury it in the back of my closet, forget it and never wear it for years. But it was there, she was real once. She was a story the rest of the time.

★ ★ ★

"Weird, isn't it?" Faiz said. "How out of all of us Brown kids, none became doctors, but this dead white lady did?"

"Why is that weird?" I asked.

"Oh, you know," he said, flustered as Sairah and I stared at him. "Because…"

Sairah and I looked at each other and started laughing. Faiz joined in nervously.

"I'm not cut out to be a doctor," I said. "I was atrocious at science."

"And math," Sairah joined in.

"Yeah. I wasn't cut out to be an architect either," I said. "So here I am doing research and looking at old buildings."

"And ghosts," Faiz said.

"And getting nowhere," I said.

"Maybe the only person who knows what happened to Carolyn is Carolyn?" Sairah said.

"Good, mission accomplished. Let's go see a movie," Faiz said.

"It would be nice if she had this one piece of information to herself," I said. "But I want to know so badly. I wish we could just talk to her. Too bad we can't summon ghosts."

"No, we should be grateful," Faiz said.

"I still have the Ouija board," Sairah said suddenly and quietly.

"No… no, no," Faiz said, alarmed, shaking his head.

"I thought you got rid of it after what happened last time," I said.

"It's still in my attic," Sairah said.

"And it'll stay there," Faiz said.

Sairah stared at me. I thought for a second. "Don't tell me you're seriously considering this!" Faiz said. I held up a finger to silence him.

"I think it's best," I said. "If we just leave her alone. I mean not alone, alone, but if we stick to the books."

"And the facts," Sairah said. "I don't know, Laana, that sounds pretty scientific to me."

★ ★ ★

In some ways the past is glaring at us. Decisions that were made hundreds of years ago still have consequences today.

Words get divorced from their original meanings. They change and morph and become different things. Everyone forgets where they came from.

What we know to be true changes over time. There were things we believed a hundred years ago that we would laugh at now. A hundred years is enough time to disprove, to refute, to debunk, to discover, to change, to learn, to grow. What we think to be fact now will be fiction someday.

Time isn't a river, but a lake or an ocean or maybe a pond. Maybe it's just a pool of water. Maybe it's a creek near a hill.

Chapter 5

The next day, after returning some books to the library (few mentions of Carolyn's job or education, but plenty of her childlessness), I went for an unplanned walk through the cemetery. The air was cold enough to sting my cheeks a little, but I kind of liked it.

I walked by the gravestones slow enough to read all the names, knowing they didn't belong to people who looked like me or Sairah or Taylor, but to people who were, in many ways, like Carolyn – white, wealthy, given some historical importance, part of the image of the town, gone.

I, with all of my navigational weaknesses, was now able to find my way around the cemetery. I walked to an area on top of the slope, where there were statues of what people called "prominent" members of the town's "founding" families. I would argue having statues made of them is the very thing that made them prominent.

I could think of plenty of people we knew who had done as much for this town as these people did who were not going to be given statues, who wouldn't appear in textbooks or plaques, whose houses were already gone.

★ ★ ★

Next to me, I could hear the rustling of pages as Sairah and Faiz went through their boxes. I paused and put mine down.

"She did so much, devoted her life to curing people. She practically, or even actually, gave her life to this town, and what?" I asked. "All she gets is a plaque?"

"A nurse who couldn't save herself," Sairah said.

"I mean, she wasn't that good a nurse," Faiz said.

We both snapped our heads to glare at him.

"Are you serious?" I asked.

"She died from contracting a disease. She was a nurse. She should have been able to treat herself, or at the very least she shouldn't have gotten sick in the first place!" he exclaimed.

"They didn't have the science or tools we have now. The illnesses were more deadly. And obviously a nurse is more likely to get sick," Sairah said.

"Do you ever think about how many of her patients could have been cured with the stuff we have now?" I asked. "Or Carolyn. If she had gotten sick today, she probably would have recovered. All these people just had the misfortune of being born at the wrong time, when something we can solve with a prescription was fatal."

"For them, that was as far as they had gotten," Sairah said. "They probably could never imagine how different things are now."

"Some deaths feel avoidable in some way, right?" I asked. Like there were things someone could have done. As if there are avoidable deaths. As if we have some control. I guess there's always some sort of bargaining that happens.

"I wonder what it's like to be surrounded by all that death," I said. "Carolyn probably had a completely different perspective on it."

"I wonder if she could detach herself from it," Sairah said. "Or if she got somewhat desensitised to it."

"That's a question. Laana, do you get used to thinking about it all the time?" Faiz asked.

"Not really. I just want to learn more. I have even more questions. I don't get bored of it. I don't feel like stopping. You know, I thought things would be different now, but it's not. I still want to learn and talk and read about it. It's not entirely this sad and difficult thing. It's still a complicated unknown."

★ ★ ★

Sairah walked into my room to find me sitting on the floor with stacks of books towering over me and pages fanning out in rows away from me. She carefully made her way over, stepping on the few patches of bare floor between me and the door.

Once she got next to me, she didn't say anything, just surveyed the papers and books. I continued to look at the old map of Clifton in my lap.

"All these books on the history of Clifton," she said, "and not one that isn't by a white guy."

I held up a copy of *Nursing in the Northeast*, not moving my eyes from the map. "This one's by a woman."

"A whole book," Sairah said. "Progress."

I continued to study the map. Then I looked up. "You know, I hadn't really thought much about that. I guess I should have."

Sairah took a seat next to me. "I just wonder who's going to write about us, you know? There are no books on us, on our parents. Our community isn't mentioned in here, or in our textbooks. And I just worry what they're going to say when they do get around to writing about us. They're probably going to say we weren't allowed to wear what we wanted to and had to stay indoors all the time."

"There's not much to do around here anyway," I joked.

"You've seen all of the textbooks and the museums. Indigenous people aren't in those books either, neither are Black people, as if the white people just stumbled across this plot of empty land and built a whole town here by themselves. We'll be erased too."

"We didn't have to go through that, either."

"Someone will find some way to change what we did go through. Even if we go down in history, we're not going down the right way."

★ ★ ★

"You have to see this," I said, turning my laptop towards Faiz. The screen showed a blog dedicated to ghost sightings around Clifton. Only one entry had mentioned Carolyn – twelve years ago.

"It looks like Carolyn's not alone," Faiz said. "There are other ghosts."

We had managed to snag one of the booths at the coffee shop and proceeded to cover the table in our belongings. I moved over so I was on the same side of the booth as Faiz. I read the words on the screen as he scrolled. I held up my hand to get him to stop, then nodded so he could scroll through. There were several ghost sightings at the cemetery. Some under the bridge at the park. One at our middle school. Several around City Hall.

On the side, there was a tab for further reading. I scanned the list. I had read all the articles and books except one: *The Haywards* by Hania Qureshi.

★ ★ ★

I searched online. Barnes & and Noble. Amazon. Goodreads. Google. eBay. Nothing came up. I even joined some local buy- and- sell Facebook groups. Still nothing. Not even an acknowl- edgement that it existed. "No search results" every time. There was just one hit on Google, in a reference for one of the books I already had.

The Haywards didn't leave a trace.

★ ★ ★

Faiz called.

"Laana," he said. "You'll never guess who runs that blog."

"How did you find out?"

"Daiam told me. He knew."

★ ★ ★

"It's you?" I said.

"You were expecting someone… different?" Taylor said with a smirk.

"Not expecting," I said. "Just hypothesising. What happened to letting the past go?"

"This isn't about the past," she said. "People think they're seeing the ghosts now."

"But what's the point of logging them all?"

"I was trying to see what was happening. I was kind of interested in where the ghost sightings took place The idea that a certain place was reminding people of something or was really scary, and I guess I really like old things. As I always say –"

"There's always precedents," I said, finishing her sentence.

"One October everyone who came in was talking about ghosts. There were so many of them. Sometimes it was a creepy location. Sometimes it was a creepy person. So, it got me thinking, what were these places and who were these people? So, I started a blog."

"When did you start it?"

"I must have been seventeen, eighteen."

"How did you get the book?"

"I played in a band with Faiz's brother, Daiam. He borrowed it from our other friend, Wren, who loaned it to me when I started the blog. But I gave it back to him after."

"I don't think I know him. Is he still here?"

"Nah, he moved to California for college like ten years ago."

"And his family?"

"Moved to Jersey two years after that."

"Ugh," I hung my head. "You know that book's near impossible to find. It's not at the library or the bookstores."

"Excellent," she said happily, while I stared at her in puzzled exasperation. "A challenge."

★ ★ ★

I walked rapidly into V's, the burger place, the door swinging behind me as I strode up to Faiz and Sairah's table.

"Hey, how did —" Faiz said.

"What did Wren's family do with their things before they moved away?" I interjected.

"Laana, you could manage, like, ten seconds of small talk instead of catching people off-guard with questions like that right out the gate." Sensing that he was otherwise occupied, Sairah exploited the situation by swiping a fry from his plate.

"My inability to make small talk is by far the least concerning thing about me. I'm tracking down a ghost," I responded while Sairah took another fry.

"You need to ease into the ghost talk," Faiz said.

"I think it's endearing," Sairah countered.

"I don't have time for easing into things," I said. "What happened to Wren's books?"

"How am I supposed to know?" Faiz asked. "What would you do with a book if you moved?"

"Give it to Sairah," I said, at the same time Sairah said, "Give it to Laana."

Faiz let out an annoyed huff.

"But what do people do with books they don't want?" Sairah asked.

"Donate them to the library?" I asked. "But I already checked there." I slumped into the booth.

Sairah offered me a fry from Faiz's plate. I took it reluctantly.

"Okay, but other than the library, what's a place that has books people don't want anymore?" she asked.

My eyes widened. "Mr. Brooks'," I said.

"No," Faiz said. "That place is haunted!"

"What, you're afraid of some books?" Sairah asked.

"Don't you guys remember Halloween?" Faiz said.

"Which Halloween?" I asked.

"Ninth grade, I think," Faiz said. "We were all there. So was Devon."

"Oh, so the last time we all hung out?" Sairah said.

Faiz raised his eyebrows at her. "I'm sorry, but the blame is mutual."

"It wasn't Devon. But Amara was there," Sairah said.

"I don't think it was Halloween," I said. "It was the day after."

"Nah, I'm fairly certain it was on Halloween," Faiz said. "That's why it was so spooky."

"No, it was the day after, that's why it was so scary," I said. "If it was Halloween, we would have assumed it was just another prank. Also, what would we be doing in a used bookstore on Halloween?"

"Because it's haunted!" Faiz said.

"It wasn't the bookstore. But we went to the bookstore before. I can see where the confusion happened," she said to Faiz, deliberately patronising.

"Okay, so where do you think it was?" Faiz said.

"Moon Diner," Sairah said.

"Moon?" Faiz said.

"I thought that closed down," I said.

"It's now called Eggceptional," Faiz said.

"Oh no, we're not –" I said.

"See you both at 11:00am on Saturday," Sairah said.

I groaned.

"Not so fast, you know. You'll need to see if you can get a reservation," Faiz said with a slight smirk.

Sairah's jaw slowly dropped.

"This just gets worse and worse," she muttered, pulling out her phone.

★ ★ ★

Being in what was once Moon made me furious. The structure was still the same. The windows were the same shape – pointed at the top with a decorative grille, so that it looked like it belonged to a paper cut-out dollhouse. But instead of the walls being painted dark red, green, blue, and black, now everything was painted white, accented by pastel vases and small jars on large, mostly empty shelves. The room was brighter, well-lit, like an ultra-modern furniture store, but it was also colder, impersonal, clinical.

There were no ghosts here. They had been driven away.

But there were no demons either. They had been erased.

As the waiter showed us to our table, I stared at the surroundings, feeling both shocked and alienated. Faiz looked lost. Sairah looked bitter.

Because the windows were still the same shape, the memories remained. If it had been dark outside, it would have been easier to remember. They came back fractured: a larger-than-average wooden red and black toy train, a piercing but short scream, a pale figure in the window, the sound of glass breaking, Sairah storming out.

"I miss the train that would run along the top of the bar," I said. They both looked up at what was now a mirror. Sairah looked back down at the menu and took a sip of her water.

"There was a train there?" Faiz asked, incredulously.

We both nodded.

"I never noticed."

* * *

In psychology class they made us watch this video where someone is talking at you on a sidewalk while people walk around in the background. It's a transition video – they're explaining to you how what you just saw is going to link up to what you're about to see and the whole time you have no idea they're experimenting on you. Because once the presenter finishes their monologue, they look at the camera and say, "Did you see the dinosaur?"

They replay the clip, and you see that in the background, figures dressed in giant rabbit, duck, bear, and even a dinosaur costume had walked by as the presenter was talking. And you missed them. You were oblivious.

You can't exactly tell the presenter you were giving them the respect of paying attention and it took so much energy and effort to focus that you had to tune everything else out, including whatever costumes were in the background. You need to filter out the noise at whatever cost. You're good at blocking out details. You've learned how to avoid what you need to.

Sairah turned to me. "Laana, now that we've done our research, what's your verdict?" she asked. "What do you think happened?"

I looked at her blankly. When we first walked into the diner, I saw everything the way Faiz described. When I heard Sairah order a milkshake, a shudder ran down my spine. I heard her telling us a ghost story, and I heard fourteen-year-old Faiz's scream.

I didn't want to fill in the blanks.

"Why can't you both be right?" I muttered.

"What's the whole point of everything you've been doing?" Sairah asked.

"You really want to talk about a fight you and Faiz had almost ten years ago?" I asked. Faiz looked embarrassed.

I remembered everything.

"It wasn't a fight," Sairah said.

"Oh really? Then why haven't the two of you haven't talked in so long?"

★ ★ ★

We heard a yell and a thud. Jay, covered in a white bed sheet, had jumped out from behind a shelf in the bookstore. Sairah, in front of him, didn't even flinch. Faiz was his accomplice, embedded in our group, feigning fear, erupting in laughter with Jay. We weren't fazed really, but at that point Sairah was the only one of us open-minded enough to understand that the world existed outside the realm of her experience and was brave enough to admit she believed in ghosts.

"You're always making fun of me," Sairah yelled at Faiz.

He was laughing. "You gotta admit, it's pretty funny," he said.

"That wasn't funny. It was mean."

"I can't believe you fell for that," Faiz said and stopped laughing. "Guess you're not as smart as we all thought." Jay joined in the laughing.

Sairah's mouth and eyes widened as the information began to connect in her mind. She was faster than the rest of us. "So that's what this is about? You're mad about my grade on the science test? It's not my fault you failed." Sairah and Faiz had been neck-and-neck for top grades in science – until that morning, when we got our tests back and the latest set of scores had knocked Faiz down, securing Sairah's lead. I don't remember what my score was. I'm sure it was neither good nor bad. I'm sure it was unremarkable.

It was Faiz's turn to be affronted. "I didn't fail. And you cheated."

"I did not!"

It was, and still is, a baseless accusation. Sairah really was that good at science, and every other subject.

★ ★ ★

I never realised how little I paid attention to other peoples' footwear until I went shoe shopping. Then, I noticed everything: size, shape, colour, make, style, material, whether they shine, whether they look new or worn.

It's sort of similar to the way my friends thought I would see a ghost after all my research. Faiz said I was just spooking myself out, but to be honest I think it was scaring him. He was jumpier.

Sairah was different. She said I was opening myself up to it. That I was inviting it. That by taking an interest in Carolyn, she would take one in me.

I didn't think we had that much influence.

* * *

Nobody spoke until the waiter finished taking our order.

"We didn't stop hanging out because of that fight," Faiz said. "Some people just grow apart."

"It's fine. Let's not bring it up right now," Sairah said.

"Why do I remember a glass breaking?" I said.

Sairah looked shocked. Disarmed even. Faiz lowered his eyes.

"I remember you telling a story," I asked Sairah. "What was it?"

"Bloody Mary," Faiz said.

"That wasn't it," I said. "It was…" I paused, allowing the name to float into my brain, materialise out of thin air. "It was something related to the Salem Witch Trials."

Sairah nodded, avoiding my gaze.

I changed targets. "And it freaked you out," I said to Faiz. He was united with Sairah in his response, if not in anything else.

"And then I remember…" I tried to piece the next parts together. "A ghost?"

Faiz seemed to visibly shiver. I pointed at the window. "There?"

"Fine," Faiz said. "I think it was Jay or something, but I was so freaked out. I thought I saw a ghost and I screamed."

"And you knocked over the glass by accident?" I asked. Faiz stared at me, eyes wide, frozen in shock. "I honestly don't remember who did it." Faiz turned to Sairah.

"It was me," Sairah said. "I did it out of anger. Happy?"

"Not at all," I said.

"And then Sairah stormed out," Faiz said.

"We don't have to keep going," I said.

"You ran after me and we went home and ate ice cream until your parents came," Sairah said. "You stood up for me."

"I ran after you because you were my ride," I said. "And my cover."

"What?" Sairah asked.

"I wasn't supposed to be out," I said. "I told my parents I was at your house studying."

"On Halloween?" Sairah asked. "They bought that?"

"I never gave them any reason to doubt me," I took a sip of my coffee. "And I wasn't going to."

"It was Jay's idea," Faiz whispered. "It wasn't mine."

"I don't care," Sairah said, eyes narrowed.

"It doesn't matter," I added. "As long as you did nothing to stop him, you're still guilty."

★ ★ ★

We walked back through the park in silence, awkwardly piecing together the answers from brunch with our memories. Not memories necessarily, but whatever emotions had permeated through time. The fear when I walked through the park. The anger when I looked out that window. The shame when I heard the chime in the entrance of Moon sound twice.

No one wanted to be the person to dismiss past pain, or who couldn't let go of old grudges. So, we walked on, stuck between the facts of the past and the tensions of the present. But most of all, just trapped.

My mind played the events of that Halloween back in reverse, as if I was rewinding a tape, retracing our steps. Then something occurred to me.

"I hate to do this," I said. "But would you guys mind if we stopped at Brooks'?"

Both Sairah and Faiz stopped and looked at me. "You've got to be kidding me," Sairah said.

★ ★ ★

Sairah and I started coming to Mr. Brooks' Books in middle school. We spent most of our time reading those days and were tearing through novels. That was the last time we had so much time to read. Sairah had gotten really into writing in her books, which ruled out the library. I was bored with the library, having gone so often as a kid with my mom. We were burning through our allowance with all the new books we were buying from the other stores. Then, we discovered Brooks'. Everything was second-hand, so it was cheap. It would be the same thing with vinyl in a few years. And when we got older, it saved us some money on textbooks, because the same books were cycled through the curriculum and through the town. I think at one point I somehow ended up with Taylor's copy of *Frankenstein*.

"I think it might be here," I said, walking into the store and immediately darting over to one of the shelves. "I mean, this is the perfect place. Where else could it be?"

"Uh, a million other places," Faiz said. "In a compost heap. Recycled into a coffee cup. At the bottom of a donation box. Decomposed in the ground. Literal ash."

"Does anyone remember where local history was?" I asked.

"This place has a local history section?" Sairah asked.

"Of course it does," I said.

"This place is local history," Faiz said.

I quickly browsed the shelves.

"Wow, those cobwebs look so realistic," Sairah said.

"They're real," I said. "This place is ancient."

"Oh good, you'll feel right at home," she said.

"You don't come here anymore?" I asked.

She shook her head. "I don't really read old books anymore."

"I don't really read fiction at all anymore."

"Weird," she said. "You always loved it so much. More than me. I think I preferred writing."

I walked around the narrow, uneven shelves. I could remember why we would come here on Halloween. Even though, as I now remembered, Brooks refused to decorate for any holidays. Lucky for him, the place was creepy enough. Absently, I wondered what happened to him, but then I remembered why I was there. The floors were creaky, and the rooms felt like a network of tunnels. It was built like a collage of different-sized rooms, put together in a haphazard way, not unlike the way we built forts from discarded cardboard boxes as kids. The ground wasn't level, so there were often awkwardly sized steps between rooms and sometimes the ceiling would suddenly become lower or the ground would rise and fall. Despite the architectural chaos, I could always find what I needed. I weaved my way through the rooms. Faiz followed.

I heard a bump. Faiz mumbled, "Ow," and rubbed his head.

"I'm guessing you haven't been here in a while?" I asked with a smile.

"Why would I?" he replied, irritated.

I walked slowly sideways, eyeing the faint, peeling laminated labels for each section: Political Science, Psychology, Sociology. Still the wrong section.

Sairah caught up to us. I ran to another section, being careful to duck under a low ceiling.

As I wandered into the back room, I remembered bits of that Halloween. A scream. Faiz and Sairah yelling. Jay laughing in the corner across from where I was standing. The sounds echoed in my head across the years, the phantom cries sending shudders down my back. I made a right and walked to the history section.

I crouched down and focused my attention on a shelf labelled "Local History". I scanned the shelves. The books were not in alphabetical order by last name. Or by first name. The titles didn't seem to follow any particular order. But there, in the bottom right corner, the third-to-last book on the shelf was *The Haywards*.

I pulled at it in spurts, and grunted triumphantly when I finally freed the book from the shelf. I waved it in the air as I called to Sairah and Faiz.

They came from opposite directions. They didn't look at each other.

"Oh good," Sairah said quietly.

Faiz was staring at his feet. "Let's get out of here," he said. "This place makes my skin crawl."

Sairah didn't move. She was holding a copy of *Little Women*, eyes widened in shock, jaw slightly open. Her fingertips gingerly kept the cover suspended, as if unable to decide whether to keep it open or closed. I let out a sigh, mildly annoyed that her find had upstaged mine.

I took it from her hands, turned it to face me and opened the front cover. Inside, someone had written a note in familiar handwriting. My handwriting. Circa sixth grade.

It read:

> *Dear Sairah,*
> *Happy 12th birthday to my bestest friend in the whole world! Thanks for being an even better friend than I ever could have asked for and I know we're going to be partners in crime forever. I hope you have an awesome day, and I hope you like this present.*
> *Love,*
> *Laana*

It wasn't any use to me now. I turned and walked towards the front of the store. Sairah and Faiz followed.

Sairah started, "I'm so –"

I stopped and turned to face them. "No," I said. "No apologies. I was wrong, some of this stuff shouldn't be dug up. It was a long time ago. This isn't doing us any good." I took a deep breath. "We're good now." And I kept walking.

★ ★ ★

A physicist named Igor Dmitriyevich Novikov developed a theory about time travel, which said that you can't create a time travel paradox. According to the Novikov self-consistency principle, you can't change the past in any material way. Any outcomes created by time travel would only contribute to or reinforce what actually happened. So, if you went back in time to stop an event from happening, you would either fail or your actions would contribute to the actual event. So, time travel is embedded in the existing historical narrative.

A static fate.

That's the thing, right? You always end up in the same place.

★ ★ ★

I didn't open up *The Haywards* until the next morning, when I went to get some work done at Sairah's house. It had chapters on every Hayward up to Carolyn. It started with her great-grandfather, who was one of the first people to come to the town.

I flipped to the chapter on Carolyn's mother. Her family hadn't been as wealthy as her husband's. She was a governess before she got married. She helped her daughter with her studies and, if she was anything like my mother, encouraged Carolyn's love of science.

I scanned down the page until I reached the last few paragraphs:

> *Annabelle and Charles went on a trip to Chicago. It is likely they fell sick on the journey. Many historians believe they contracted either cholera or scarlet fever. Charles died within three days of reaching Chicago. Annabelle died at the end of her first week there.*
>
> *They were survived by their then thirty-three-year-old daughter Carolyn, the last member of their family.*

I turned to the chapter called "Carolyn":

Carolyn Hayward was born in October 1853. She had taken an interest in nursing from a young age, ever since her parents built the hospital. A bright child, she enjoyed her visits to the hospital and spent as much time as she could there, trying to learn.

She completed nursing school at the age of twenty-one and moved back to Clifton to work at her parents' hospital. She introduced new treatments and helped make the management more efficient and coordinated. She established a special wing in the hospital devoted to children and infants.

Many sources claim that Charles and Annabelle Hayward died during a fire in their home, but they actually died after contracting an illness during a trip. Sources disagree about the date they died but it was somewhere between 1879 and 1881. Carolyn Hayward had full ownership of the hospital and Hayward Manor following the death of her parents, and took over management of the hospital.

At the age of thirty-three she contracted an illness, most likely tuberculosis. One physician said, after reading her symptoms in a newspaper article, that it resembled malaria. Many believe she also died in a fire, or during the same fire her parents died in, but this is incorrect. Some also believe she died by suicide, but newspaper and police reports at the time ruled it out.

In addition, several reports confirm that Carolyn had next to no visitors in her home. She worked long hours every day, but rarely had people over or hosted social events at her house. Her journals state that she spent most of her evenings alone, reading medical texts. This means the rumour that she was treating patients at home was also largely unsubstantiated. She likely picked up an illness or infection from a patient of hers at the hospital.

"Find anything?" Sairah asked, looking up from her notebook.

"There wasn't a fire," I said.

We looked at each other for a moment.

"So people just made it up?" I said. Smoke out of thin air.

"Sounds about right," she scoffed.

★ ★ ★

Our psychology and history teachers told us on multiple occasions that history is not a social science. It is not a science at all, because you can't do experiments. And because you can't do experiments, you can't find or establish – or that crucial word, prove – causal relationships.

But that didn't stop history from trying. So many times we sat in class trying to explain what combinations of factors caused an economy to collapse, what theories explained why "the world" (not the full world, but what a lot of people thought was the only part of the world that mattered) went to war, whose interpretation of history we thought provided the best context.

We never got to how each historian had erased, rearranged, glossed over, omitted, compressed, squeezed, cut in half, reinterpreted, and pasted events to prove what they were trying to say. And how we were summarising and paraphrasing what they said.

★ ★ ★

I opened up *The Haywards*, and paused briefly on the foreword, which I usually skipped:

> *I grew up in Clifton. My family is made up of immigrants, like much of the community now is. Like many of the children in Clifton, I've heard stories of Carolyn Hayward's ghost since childhood. I tried to trace the origins of those stories.*

My research led me to believe that the rumours about Carolyn Hayward had started around the time of her death.

She was an intriguing figure who captured the public's attention because, other than her family's influence, her profession and connection to the hospital, not much was known about her. She was a woman who lived and, essentially, died alone. Her life was sensationalised instead of celebrated for what it was.

This book was intended to change that.

I thought of my parents' house, my grandmother's grave, the foreign-sounding names on gravestones, Moon, Carolyn's house – the markers of the life I knew would slowly erode, the landscape of my childhood resigned to memory. All traces of me someday erased, left behind in the people who outlived me, mere fragments, no physical trace. Like I was never here at all. Like I never existed. A figment of their imagination – a version of me that wasn't really me at all.

Chapter 6

I don't know how I'm supposed to think about home any more than I'm supposed to think about anyone I knew or didn't know who is now gone. How am I supposed to feel when I go for walks to places I used to and everything is either completely the same or entirely different, like I'm walking through history and also fiction, like I've been here forever and I've never been here before, and while I walk I remember what happened there, recall things I wanted to forget, relive some of my most embarrassing mistakes, feel the rush from the fun I had all those years ago, only to feel sad again when it fades away. What am I supposed to make of Carolyn, when all I have is a collection of facts and depending on how much I've read, either a lot of details or close to none about her death and very little about her life?

How am I supposed to feel about anyone when I don't know enough about them, when I never knew them or knew them well enough, and I learn new things that challenge my entire idea of who they were? How am I supposed to move on when we're all hung up on something that happened a decade ago? How am I supposed to hold all these contradictions in my mind and not spend all this time unravelling and reorganising and dissecting it?

★ ★ ★

From *New England's Architecture Through the Ages*, "Chapter Thirty-One: Hayward Manor":

Hayward Manor had twelve bedrooms, two kitchens, four studies, six lounges, a ballroom, and a library that was two stories high. Most of the contents of the library were, according to Carolyn Hayward's will, donated to a nearby school, which later became the Clifton campus of the University of Connecticut, but she also stipulated that all medical and scientific texts were to be donated to her alma mater, the Connecticut College of Nursing.

★ ★ ★

My parents didn't look up from their grading when I walked into the study. I started scanning the bookshelves.

"Do you need help?" Mom asked after a few minutes. "What are you looking for?"

"Laana, last time you borrowed a book you accidentally took it to college for a semester," Dad said.

"I brought it back, didn't I?" I said. "Unlike a certain record of mine which was living in this room for years. Anything about Clifton."

"As in —" Mom said.

"As in, yes, the ghost," I replied.

Dad sighed.

"Aren't you happy I'm taking an interest in local history?" I asked.

"Local history, yes. 'Interest' isn't the word I would use," Dad said. "Actually, neither is 'history'."

"Was this always here?" I asked. They both turned to me. I was holding a copy of a book called *Clifton: A History*. It was leather-bound, dark red, with the title embossed in chipped gold. It reminded me of Nani's copies of *Northanger Abbey* and *Rebecca*, which my mother had now, also sitting somewhere on this bookcase.

"No, actually," Dad said. "We found those books in Daadi's things."

I was there the day we packed up her house, where she lived with my aunt, an hour away, past the university. My aunt was moving now there was no reason for her to stay. But the house was just like Daadi left it. I felt we were trespassing, like she was going to come back from the grocery store any moment and be shocked that we were there and feel bad that she didn't bring us enough food, even though there was always plenty at her house.

"Can I read it?"

"Yeah," he nodded. "Laana, just –"

Mom cut in. "You know if you want to talk about anything, we're here."

"Thanks, Mom. But I'm fine. I just… need to get back to my research."

★ ★ ★

The history books all talked about Carolyn's family – or lack of family. But they never mentioned any friends or co-workers, or even patients. Not even the people who must have also lived in the big house, taking care of it and her.

Nothing about what she was like as a person. No mention of hobbies or fears or interests. Not even a sliver of an interaction with a patient. In my mind, I patched up the gaps, grafting a memory onto a composite of facts, a made-up person. I imagined she had a good sense of humour, like my doctor when I was little, constantly joking with her patients to distract them from their ailments. Always smiling, like she didn't deal with horrors every day.

★ ★ ★

"Mom, do you believe in ghosts?" I asked.

"I think they could exist," she said. "I'm not sure they do, but I'm not sure they don't. We don't have much concrete evidence that they exist, but we also can't prove they don't. There's so much about the world we don't know. That's what's so exciting about exploring and researching. In the future, they might have explanations for ghost encounters. We don't know what they are right now."

After a pause I asked, "Do we have any more local history books lying around?"

She laughed and shook her head. "There's lots of stuff at the university library that the public library doesn't have," she said. "You could try there."

"You think so?"

"I don't know what's there, but it's worth a look."

"You don't think it's weird, all of this research?"

"It's just research, the same thing you and I do all day anyway. There are worse ways you could pass the time. Mainly I'm just happy you're not bored here."

"But ghosts?"

She vanished my concern with a wave of a hand. "One more thing we have in common."

★ ★ ★

In school they give you all these diagrams and metaphors to explain your brain. Here's an anatomical representation, now fill it out like a physical map, but to represent your fleeting thoughts. Here's a flowchart that shows how things move from your immediate observations to things you think about to things you remember. They tell you your brain functions a lot like a computer, that they can teach a computer to think like you.

Your mind is an operating system, it's a filing system, it's your own worst enemy, it's your best friend, it's an organ, it's a little voice, it's a loud voice, it's a house, it's a mansion, it's actually a record player stuck on a loop, it's a collection of thoughts, those thoughts are not you, they come and go, like cars on a highway, don't let one of them carry you away, count your breaths, focus on your body. Your mind is not a prison, but your body is. And does that make your soul a prisoner? And does that make death a kind of freedom?

★ ★ ★

From *Nursing in the Northeast*, page 161:

> *Carolyn Hayward's contribution to nursing was to show that children could benefit from specialised care and attention, and to standardise the practice of having dedicated areas and staff specifically for children's healthcare, after having instituted these changes at Hayward Hospital in Clifton, Connecticut.*

★ ★ ★

"It's like you blink and ten years have gone by," I said, turning to face Sairah as she drove to the university. The wind grazed the top of my head in sharp bursts, but I didn't mind. "Ninth grade was ten years ago now."

"No," she said, turning to me briefly. "Stop!"

I gestured towards the road. She waved me off. "It feels… like it was not even two years ago. Maybe five? But definitely not ten."

"It's been twelve years since I got my braces off. Seventeen years since I learned how to ride a bike. It's been eighteen years since we met," I said.

"Okay, you need to stop doing that. Those numbers don't feel real."

"Can you feel time go by? Do you really feel that much different now than you did in ninth grade? I mean I feel different, but how much?"

"You moved away. I stayed here. You can't feel change when it's gradual."

"But what actually changed? I still have the same interests. I'm not that much different, personality-wise. I think you aren't either. We still get along."

"I like to think I've gotten better. Like I'm a revised version of myself. All of the same ideas and main themes are still there, but stuff has changed."

"So much has happened. So much time has passed. And yet it feels like it hasn't."

★ ★ ★

When we entered the university library, I presented the visitor's pass Mom had got me. They let Sairah in as an alum.

The library was, in a word, huge. There were several stories, spiral staircases and archways. And so many books. Books covering every surface. It was like the library was built from books, as if the architect didn't want even an inch of wall to be visible. It reminded me of the library I saw at a friend's university when I visited during her year abroad. I never thought I would see one so close to home. I was shocked I didn't remember it, didn't even know it had existed and this whole time it was right here.

There were shelves upon shelves of books about ancient history, describing events four, five, six hundred years ago, even more: eleven hundred, twelve hundred. Whatever information remained came from a certain kind of person – they couldn't possibly account for all experiences. They still can't. What was the value in that?

Carolyn's books had been here at some point. We asked a librarian, who had never heard of her and said they didn't keep books from the 1800s.

"They must be in archives, or storage," I said.

"They're not in our records," he said, turning the desktop screen to face me.

"Maybe they got lost in a fire," Sairah smirked as we walked away.

"Imagine living here and never having heard of Carolyn," I whispered.

But more importantly, the library did have old newspaper clippings. They let me make copies to take home. That was the easy part.

Then we had to go through the actual books and see how many would be useful for us. Unfortunately, the total count was too high. The local history books took up a whole section of a wall on the third floor, eight books high and fifty across. We had to climb through two spiral staircases to get there, as though it was some secret attic filled with books that hadn't been picked up in decades.

"It's going to take a lot of wagons to get those home," Sairah said.

So, we changed tack – we'd only check out a book if it had more than a few pages of helpful information. If it didn't, we would just read those pages there and take notes. We got to work right there on the floor in front of the shelf, unwilling to carry the books down two precarious flights of stairs to where the desks were. We were mainly quiet, flipping through the books and snapping photos with our phones or scribbling notes in our leather notebooks.

"Laana," Sairah said. "It says here she died of tuberculosis. Did you see that anywhere?"

I looked down at my notes. "I have down three mentions of unspecified disease, one of typhus, two of scarlet fever and one of consumption – is that the same thing?"

"I think so," Sairah said.

"So, it's equally likely she died of scarlet fever or tuberculosis. But we can say for pretty sure she died of some illness."

"Does it matter which one?"

"I don't know."

★ ★ ★

An hour and a half later, after I had gone through three more books, Sairah suddenly spoke.

"I got another one," she said.

"Hmm?" I said quietly, finishing reading the sentence before looking up.

"Tuberculosis," Sairah said.

I looked down at my notes. "I just saw that again too. That makes four mentions."

She handed me the book. I flipped through the pages.

"I just can't believe it was so —"

"Anonymous?" Sairah finished.

"Straightforward," I finally said.

I had lost track of how long we'd been there, but the stack of books I had gone through had grown from three to eight.

"Tuberculosis," Sairah said, turning the book to face me.

"Another one?"

She nodded. "How many are we up to?"

"Six," I said, looking up at her. "That's more than any other explanation, including fire, which we know is not true."

She shook her head. "Not everything is systemic. Some tragedies are singular."

"But random? Avoidable?"

"A lot of deaths are kind of quiet and ordinary. Dying is ordinary. Everyone does it, eventually." I knew this.

"It's just… not what I expected."

"Did you want something definitive?"

"TB doesn't always result in death."

"I mean, are you sad about the answer or are you sad you've found it?"

It was not that it was general. It was not that it didn't single Carolyn out. It was not that it was a historical event or a full-on calamity. It was not the irony that a nurse was killed by a disease or through treating people.

It was that there was no story, no injustice, no fateful error. No avoidable mistake. No blame. It was a certain, final, death. Inevitable. It wasn't personal. No elaborate narrative, no outlandish tale. Just a normal, pedestrian death for someone who wasn't that at all.

"Both, I guess."

★ ★ ★

Every time someone appears on the news, another person dead, another life over, that's another friend, family member, co-worker, partner gone. A whole life, with hopes and fears and dreams and habits and pet peeves and quirks, just not there anymore. Immaterial vastness destroyed materially.

But on the news they stick to the material facts. They don't talk about life; they talk about details. They don't talk about memories; they talk about evidence. Whole lives, whole tragedies, reduced to an item on a ticker tape.

Sondering is a recent word that means you realise that other people live entire lives as messy and complicated as your own. It reminded me of another word, but I couldn't remember what it was. I asked Sairah. She said it was just common sense. It was obvious, it goes without saying. That's why there's no word for it.

★ ★ ★

"You know that's been scheduled for demolition for years, right?" Faiz said.

"So I've heard, but I only saw the sign about a month ago," I said.

"I think they put up the notice when we were in college or something," he said.

"That long ago?" I said.

"You haven't been back in a while."

"I came back during every break in college. I wasn't running around Europe or whatever."

He batted my comment away.

"I guess it's like the dinosaur," I said.

"The what now?"

"The dinosaur from the psychology video."

"Laana, context please. You're making even less sense than usual."

"There was this video in psychology class where they have people in animal costumes walk across the screen and you barely notice. Like some magic trick. Kinda like how you never noticed the train at Moon."

"It's not a magic trick. You just weren't paying attention." After a pause. he added, "Why would you? You weren't coming back. I probably wouldn't have noticed if I was just visiting."

"Why did you come back?"

"It wasn't supposed to be for this long."

"That's how it always is."

★ ★ ★

A dead writer's unused stationery sells for a quarter of a million dollars. The book Sairah's reading was published posthumously. An album came out last week by a rapper who died two years ago. I remember when she died, Taylor said she had to order extra copies of her vinyl's, CDs and cassettes because there was so much demand for them – the record companies keep finding music to sell, but the artist had struggled her entire career. On a trip to New Orleans, my friends and I took two different ghost tours because there were so many, and each was different. When I was in high school, I searched every bookstore in Clifton – yes, all three of them – trying to find a copy of this movie magazine I liked that no one else seemed to read, but it was sold out everywhere that week. A famous actress had died, her face on the cover of the magazine, smiling. I knew what it looked like, but I never actually saw a physical copy of it. I had never seen it sell out before or since.

★ ★ ★

"What, you think you're on *CSI* or something?" Faiz snickered.

"That's ridiculous," I said, not looking up from the list of symptoms of tuberculosis I had found online, trying to compare them my notes of Carolyn's diary entries. "They have much more evidence to work with. All I have are stories. What they do is a walk in the park compared to this."

"Our park is haunted," Faiz said.

"They're just stories. That's all I have, stories," I said. There are just stories we tell about people who aren't here, for whatever reason that might be: they died, they lived a long time ago, they live in another country, they've gone to the grocery store, they were just too busy to hang today. Just stories.

After a pause, Faiz asked, "Laana, you like difficult questions. Have you asked yourself why you feel the need to do all this?"

"*You* have before, at least a couple of times," I said, not looking up from my laptop.

He paced around me. "But do you know why you've become so obsessed with some random white lady who died a hundred years ago?"

"Roughly 135 years ago," I said, raising my eyes to meet his. He shot me a look. "But who's counting?" I smirked.

He let out an exasperated sigh. "Yes, I have," I said. There's no clear reason. It's even harder than figuring out how Carolyn died. There are all of the convenient, neat explanations – too obvious, too easy.

"Why?" he asked.

A million reasons flooded my mind: people are obsessed with tons of dead white ladies for lots of reasons. This town is obsessed with Carolyn's death. We've always heard the stories, but we don't know anything about her. It's our own legend, our most popular piece of history, and this is our town too, it's our ghost story. Some people like to do research and some people get carried away and I have always been both those people. I always find something to obsess about, I do lots of research and reading whenever I get interested in something. I have always been obsessed with death and I don't know why. And I don't know why we always need reasons for things.

I finally replied. "I think I needed a focus, maybe a distraction."

★ ★ ★

I went to the bookstore to buy that movie magazine. While I was there, I figured I might as well get a newspaper for my parents. On the cover was a very graphic image of people who had died, photographed in Kenya. A magazine next to it showed a laptop screen with the words, "Active shooter on campus." There were no bodies on the cover. Not a single person. If you didn't see those words, in that order, there was no death. So, this is how they protect them. So this is how much they mean to them.

★ ★ ★

"Laana, I have to ask you something," Sairah said.

"Yeah?" I said, looking up from my textbook. It was the first week of senior year of high school, and we were doing homework in Sairah's bedroom. I don't remember what homework we were doing, just that we had a lot only a few days in, much to our dismay. I don't think we got a lot done.

Sairah got up and walked over to her bed. She bent down, reached under it, and pulled out a shoebox. She took the lid off and showed me its contents: a stack of slim leather notebooks. After a deep breath, she said slowly, "I need you to promise me that when I die, you'll destroy these notebooks."

I looked at her for a second. "I have so many questions," I responded. "What's in them? How do I destroy them? With fire? Does leather even burn?"

Her expression instantly shifted from nervousness to annoyance. "I don't care how you do it. I just someone I trust" she gestured at me, "to get rid of them. To make sure nobody sees them, reads them, gets their hands on them, shares them, or publishes them. It's my writing, and I get to decide when – and how – the world gets to see it... or not."

"You got it," I said. "Whatever you need, I'll do it. I'll even delete your browser history and wipe your hard drives."

"Oh, good idea."

"Just one question."

"Sure, what's that?"

"Don't you love reading this stuff? Diaries and unfinished work by dead writers."

"That's exactly why you gotta burn it. It's too tempting. People eat it up. And you never know, I might become really famous after I die."

"What if it's the unfinished thing that makes you famous?"

"I don't want to become famous that way. It's not really my work, because I wouldn't have published something I didn't finish writing. I wouldn't really be famous, because I wouldn't be alive anymore."

"I never really thought of that... all the posthumous stuff... it wasn't finished by the author, wasn't released as intended. We'll never know what the finished product was supposed to be."

★ ★ ★

"I don't think Hayward Manor's haunted," I said.

"Why's that?" Sairah asked nonchalantly, taking a bite out of her sandwich.

"Because Carolyn can go anywhere she wants. Why would she hang around in the same place she lived for thirty years?"

"Good point," Sairah laughed. "She could be halfway to Tokyo now for all we know!"

"Nothing about ghost stories makes sense. People have all these weird ideas."

"People have lots of weird ideas about lots of people. Like us."

"You mean writers and art historians?" I joked.

Sairah laughed. "If only we could just be writers and art historians."

★ ★ ★

I took a stack of books to one of the new coffee shops near the library. I flicked through them, taking notes on what kind of student Carolyn was, what she did as a nurse, who she was as a member of the community. They mainly agreed, but disagreed here and there. One book failed to mention she was a nurse.

I looked around the coffee shop. I didn't recognise a single person. I felt relieved that I didn't have to relive high school through the unmentioned subtext of fleeting pleasantries. But also that I was surrounded by strangers. I felt surprisingly alone.

Everything about the coffee shop began to feel unfamiliar. The smooth tabletops with their sharp, rectangular edges. The bare lightbulbs hanging from the ceiling. The small chairs, the pastel cushions, the stock art in sleek frames arranged in a pattern that felt fresh yet organised. Even the coffee tasted different from what I was used to.

I returned to my book, but I was distracted by the snatches of conversations I caught, questions asked by strangers to people who weren't strangers to them, a laugh here and there, fragments of dialogue I couldn't connect to form a plot, entire storylines, entire lifetimes I would never know about. These people who shouldn't be strangers. Who were my neighbours.

I bent down further over the book, trying to focus. I wondered if I should try the bookstore nearby and made a mental note to stick to the old coffee shops next time.

Then, a familiar song came on. I was vaguely nodding my head along before I realised I had heard it before. Dozens of times.

And then suddenly, I was hearing this song for the first time when it ended up on my iPod after Amara and I did a big song exchange in high school. I was fourteen, singing along with Sairah in the car after school. I was at the mall aged fifteen, debating which jacket to wear to Sairah's birthday party. I was eighteen, complaining that Jay's taste in music was out of date when he insisted on playing it during my cursed graduation party.

I was twenty-four, wondering why a new, hip, trendy, expensive coffee shop insisted on playing pop hits from ten years ago.

A few days later, Sairah, also twenty-four years old, would say that though she had started listening to this song again ironically, she had actually grown to like it.

★ ★ ★

The bathroom looked much older than the coffee shop did. Maybe they never bothered to redo it. The stalls reminded me of the ones in high school, covered in scribbles, littered with mock-profound quotes, declarations of existence, vows for revenge. I couldn't stop staring at one message written in black Sharpie towards the bottom of the door: Carolyn Hayward came back to life.

Underneath it in blue ballpoint by someone with a shakier hand: and she is not happy about it.

★ ★ ★

"It's really weird how, according to anyone who bothered to mention it, Carolyn's patients loved her, yet all anyone talks about how is how she died," I said.

"You sound like Becca," Sairah said.

"I'm sorry, who?" I replied.

"Becca Delaney," Sairah said.

"Becca? I don't remember a Becca."

"She had long dark hair," Faiz said.

"So did more than half the school," Sairah added.

"She laughed a lot," Faiz said.

"People always say that about girls." Sairah rolled her eyes.

"Her family moved to Connecticut at the start of high school," Faiz said. "She was in my bio class."

"Thanks, that really helps me, since I never took bio," I said.

Faiz threw up his hands. "Can't win."

Sairah was gazing at him with a satisfied look on her face.

"How is it, Sairah, that you've ended up with not one, but two friends who became obsessed with the same ghost?" he shot back.

She ignored him and turned to me. "But seriously, you don't remember her?"

"No," I said. "Does anybody have a picture?" Faiz held up a finger as he pulled out his phone. "Did I ever talk to her?"

Sairah shook her head. "We didn't have any classes with her. She was on the soccer team, and mainly hung out with them."

Faiz showed me the picture. "Remember her?"

I nodded, but only to cover up the fact that this person had completely dropped out of my memory.

"She used to work at the hospital," Sairah said.

"Hayward – I mean Clifton Primary?" I asked.

"The very same," Sairah said.

"A nurse who believes in ghosts," Faiz said. "Is that what a historian would refer to as a 'reliable source'?"

"Was I a reliable source when I mixed up the deadlines for our eighth-grade final science project and we both got marked down for being late?" I said.

"That was ten years ago!"

"Do your own research!"

"But you do plenty of it for the rest of us," he said. "How did Becca get into this stuff, anyway?"

"She was interested in the founder of the hospital where she worked," Sairah said, then looked at me. "And she learned a lot about Carolyn. She moved. She's in Seattle now. But I message her sometimes on Instagram."

"I just can't believe you know someone who worked at the hospital," I said, and still couldn't conjure a face. "Okay, there's someone else, I have her face in my head, I can see her. No idea what her name is. She was in my AP Lit class senior year."

They both stared at me blankly. "Laana, how am I supposed to remember who was in your class? I can't even remember the name of my math tutor and I had him for two years," Faiz said.

"Can you remember your AP Math score?" I asked.

Sairah's jaw dropped, then a smile broke out across her face. "I knew it! I knew you had an unfair advantage."

"I'm never going to live this down now," he sighed. "It's good to ask for help when you need it."

"Why were you even taking AP Math if you needed a tutor?" I asked.

Faiz shrugged. "Looked good on a college application. And no, I don't remember my score."

Sairah looked at him for a long moment, then looked at me. "Can either of you remember your SAT scores?" she asked.

We both tried to remember for a minute, then shook our heads.

"How could I forget?" I said.

"It's not that you forgot. It's that it seemed so important in the first place," Sairah said.

★ ★ ★

I asked Becca if I could Skype her because I needed to know what she looked like. When she suddenly appeared on the screen and I heard her laugh reverberate across time zones, I remembered her. A girl sitting at the end of the cafeteria with a bright, tinkling, graceful laugh that proved to be contagious among the rest of the soccer team. Her tight curls of pitch-black hair didn't fit in the frame.

"I was fifteen when we moved to Clifton. I heard all the stories about Carolyn for the first time, and I thought Clifton was super unsafe," she laughed. "I thought it was really spooky and creepy."

I laughed. "But then you realised," I said.

"Yeah, not much happens around there," she said. "But I was relieved. I kind of liked it. Small town, everyone knows each other. Not like the big cities where you feel lost."

"I love big cities. I'm tired of my neighbours reminding me of stuff I did as a kid."

She laughed. "You look the same," she said.

"So do you. And I still get asked what grade I'm in."

"I guess it's flattering?"

"I don't think I'm old enough to feel that way."

"What did you want to know about Carolyn Hayward?"

I thought about it for a minute. "All of it. Anything you know about her."

Becca told me what she knew about Carolyn. Which nursing school she went to, when she started working at the hospital, her nursing methods, how she was good with kids and how she focused on the children's section. She even told me that, until Carolyn's death, they'd been trying to expand the children's part of the hospital. I don't know how she knew that.

"And how did she die?"

Becca laughed again. "That's the question, isn't it? Everyone talks about how she died; nobody talks about all the amazing things she did when she was alive."

"She was pretty incredible. And thank you, you've been really helpful on that front. I feel like I'm learning so much I didn't know about her."

"I'm happy you care! So, the thing is that she was definitely sick. I saw the records – the hospital kept them in the archives. She died there, not at home like everyone thought. Anyway, so looking at the records, her symptoms sounded like tuberculosis."

"TB, you sure?"

"Yeah, that's my guess. Were you thinking it was something different?"

"I've heard every possible explanation, including TB. But no one saw the hospital records. I don't know. It just feels weird… she did all this stuff, and then she died from something there's a vaccine for now."

"She feels larger than life. It's weird to think she just got sick, and that's what killed her. Not like a mythic bolt of lightning or something. That at the end of the day, she was a person, with an immune system."

"It sounds silly, but the more I read about her, the more it feels like she couldn't die. That she's still out there somewhere."

★ ★ ★

An album Taylor recommended – which she swore came out last month – sounded like another album that came out in 2005. How can I enjoy anything when everything reminds me of something else? How can I listen to a song when it sounds like a song I used to sing in the car with Amara on the way to hockey practice and that same song was playing at the pizza place we fought at post-practice? It is unfair how things can be ruined by association. It's unfair to the listener and the artist and the person it reminds them of. To be trapped, eternally preserved in a memory of you doing something wrong. To be frozen in a brief moment of antagonism. It's not who you are, but the other person will see you that way for days, years even.

Music has this weird property of immediately evoking memories. Smells do too. When one latches onto a bad memory, it's hard to separate them. Listening to the song causes you to remember, and it ruins the song for you. Taylor says to keep listening anyway, and the new memories will overwrite the bad ones, the same way you can get a song out of your head by listening to it, because you get stuck on one part and need to move past it.

Time is a loop, actually.

Chapter 7

When we were little, the park looked different. Actually, the whole town was different. We have a lot of photos of that time period. I wondered if my parents could sense things were changing, felt some need to document things as they were. We went through those photos so many times.

I can see whole stories my parents told me from my own perspective, eyes closer to the floor. Sometimes I feel like I remember what the park looked like when I went for walks with my mother, and I have vivid recollections of shop fronts that closed over two decades before. I could tell you the outline of the old playground before they rebuilt it. I remember a rickety bridge going across the creek. But then I remember the photos and all the stories my parents told me, and I wonder if what I'm remembering is the actual event, or what's left. The things designed to capture and communicate, but unable to recreate, reabsorbed as memory. Whose memory is it – mine or my parents'?

I have no idea what my earliest memory is. I only have memories of memories.

★ ★ ★

"We're going to be late," Dad said.

"When are we not?" I said, fixing my hair in the mirror. I ran to grab a jacket. "Why did we even bother making a reservation in the first place?"

"Yeah, when was the last time we ever made it anywhere on time?" Mom said.

"I blame both of you," I said.

"Very easy to blame someone else," Dad said. "But you've lived on your own for a while now. What stops you from getting to classes on time?"

"Genetics," I replied. "And, technically, I've never been marked absent." I always came in just under the fifteen-minute cut-off. Even my professors stopped commenting on it and just accepted it. My friends started telling me to arrive at places fifteen minutes before the actual time they wanted to meet.

"Never on time either," Dad said.

"We have that in common."

"Why couldn't you have inherited one of my better qualities?"

"Because of me," Mom said. "Just accept it. Everyone just needs to add five minutes to our ETA."

"Or tell us to come earlier than everyone else," Dad said.

"Five minutes? That's optimistic," I said. "At least ten, probably fifteen."

"Okay, this whole conversation is definitely bumping us up to fifteen," Dad said. "Everybody in the car."

The reservation was for 7:30 pm. We got there at 8:00 pm. "Eight is a much better time for dinner," Mom said. "Who eats dinner before eight?"

★ ★ ★

When we're not doing laps, we're putting distance in between who we are now and who we used to be. Changing interests, listening to music we've never heard before, abandoning old TV shows, picking up new hobbies, swapping out clothes, moving away, switching careers, hanging out with a different group of people. Telling people, "Oh that was me then, this is me now," conning ourselves into thinking we've grown, progressed, improved. But it's quantity over quality.

We're running away.

And there are things you can't outrun.

★ ★ ★

"Remember those choose-your-own-adventure books?" Sairah asked as we walked to the bookstore. We had both filled up our leather notebooks and needed new ones.

"They feel so outdated now," I said. "Why do that when you could play a video game or something?"

"They're still fun," Sairah replied, mock-offended. "But I never played them, I just liked to look at all the options."

"Yeah, I think I like having options. I like having multiple outcomes. It's frustrating you only get one life."

"I liked seeing the cause-and-effect. And knowing what would change what, where it went wrong."

We walked a few more steps, passing the shop where we used to buy our musical instruments.

"How's the piano going, by the way?" I asked.

"The what?" Sairah asked.

"Piano." She stopped and stared at me blankly. I stopped, now ahead of her, and had to turn around. "You played, right? You took lessons for a while?"

She laughed and started walking again. "That was a phase. A very short phase. I think it lasted, like, three months. I barely made it through my classes. Actually," she stopped again. "I'm not sure if I finished the course I was taking." She turned to me. "I'm surprised you remember."

"I thought you took lessons for years."

"Nope. I begged and begged my parents for a piano. I wanted to sing and play and write songs. And then I got it and took lessons and realised that actually I didn't want to practice and just abandoned it. I don't even have the keyboard anymore. We got rid of it at a yard sale."

"Do you ever wonder who has it now?"

"No, I don't think about it. I barely even remembered I played the piano for a while."

★ ★ ★

I scanned the bookshelf. "*Frankenstein* was written by a woman, right?" I asked. Sairah nodded. "And so was *Wuthering Heights* and so was *Jane Eyre*."

"Lots of horror books were written by women," Sairah said. "And everyone conveniently forgets."

"We're not supposed to think about violence or death – we're supposed to think about the other thing," I said. "Not that one thing should define or determine who women are."

"But no one lets us decide or listens to us," Sairah continued. "It always frustrated me how all the stories by or centred on men were larger than life and about conquering some big thing or confronting their own mortality or their own evilness. And women's stories –"

"Are about marriage or motherhood," I finished her sentence. About other people.

"But these women wrote about violence and loss and horror, and weren't afraid to be dark, to confront death, to write about ugliness, to create the grotesque."

"They weren't scared, and they weren't afraid of making you scared."

"You know *Frankenstein* was considered the first science-fiction book?"

"And science-fiction is seen as such a male thing." I thought of my mother and her textbooks and her books of scary stories.

"And then instead of talking about all their great contributions, people love focusing on these writers' deaths. Never mind all the stuff they wrote, all people want to talk about is the horrible tragedies they went through."

When we read poems in school, all anyone would talk about was the writers' struggles with mental illness – because, of course, women are always thought to be too emotional, as if there wasn't anything else going on in their lives, as if there weren't other things they could have written about, as if there wasn't more to them, as if they weren't other things. But you get remembered for one thing, and that's all you are. Women are often one thing: pretty, smart, crazy, depressed, evil – never more than one.

"We're not allowed to do anything that makes us stand out," I said. You get punished for being the slightest bit different.

"When women are creative or intelligent or successful, they're crazy, never reasonable, never a genius," Sairah said. "And what it does is make you afraid of your own intelligence or ambition or creativity because it's a sign of madness. We're always afraid of going crazy. Of feeling too much because we're branded as emotional, defined by it to the point that it's seen as dangerous – even to us. Men get to create and it's a great thing. But women just create and die. And if they're too smart, they get burnt at the stake."

"Or become a vengeful ghost."

* * *

From *Carolyn Hayward: A Biography*, page 112:

> *Having visited the hospital since she was a child, Carolyn wanted the care of children to be emphasised. She hired extra nurses specifically to look after children, and dedicated two wards for infants, three for children under twelve and one specifically for teenagers. She also expanded the maternity ward.*

* * *

I don't know if anyone ever proved that a butterfly could start a hurricane. Maybe it's just a myth, a suburban legend. Pure fiction. Maybe it was just a metaphor, a catchy title.

But sometimes, in thinking, in sifting through events, you find a chain reaction. A set of dominos. Things you did years ago that you are still feeling the effects. How many random ideas and split-second decisions are responsible for completely changing your path, taking you off one course and onto another? How many times can you trace a big event back to a smaller decision that happened years ago, like moving inwards from the outer ripples or counting back from the rings of a tree.

And I can see it, I can see the rings and the ripples. I can count all the dots. And you can draw flowcharts alleging any major event is connected to some small, seemingly insignificant occurrence.

If I hadn't chosen band instead of choir, I would never have met Amara. And if I hadn't met Amara, we wouldn't have ridden our scooters together after school. And if we didn't ride our scooters, I wouldn't have that scar on my leg from when I fell over. But if I hadn't fallen over, Mom wouldn't have come to pick me up, and she wouldn't have started talking to Amara's mom and older sister, and maybe Amara's sister wouldn't have wanted to become an engineer. Or maybe my mom had nothing to do with it. That was the day when Amara found out she couldn't stand the sight of blood and so couldn't become a doctor. And so she ended up going to business school, left Clifton and never came back.

And if I had made the basketball team, we probably would have been closer. And if we hadn't chosen universities that were so far away from each other, we wouldn't have drifted apart.

★ ★ ★

"You know, *The Very Last Ending* was on TV last night," I said. "And I hadn't seen it since we went to see it back in eighth grade at the Cineplex. And I remembered everything you said. Every comment, joke and question."

"I remember that too," Faiz said. "Because that was one of the first times I was allowed to go to the movies by myself." He paused. "What did you think?"

"I liked it so much better this time. I guess back then I didn't like thrillers as much, or didn't get them, or maybe I was too young, or whatever."

He laughed. "Have you seen *The Very First Beginning*?" he asked.

I stared at him for a second. "Yeah! You were there! You made me watch it with you! All of us. At your house. We made nachos. Well, more like we made a mess and there were nachos there."

He looked down at the ground and frowned. "Weird. I don't remember that. At all…"

"I forgot that we used to hang out all the time at one point. Because we stopped. I barely saw you in high school. But before that we saw movies all the time."

"They say that theatre is haunted."

"The Cineplex? I've never heard that."

"Not the Cineplex as a whole. That room where we saw *The End*."

I opened my mouth to speak, but before I could get a word out, Faiz held up his hand and said. "No. Absolutely not."

"You didn't even give me a chance to talk."

"I know that look." He let out a dramatic sigh. "I know where we're going."

★ ★ ★

"Laana," Faiz yelled. "Once again, may I ask why we are scouting out potentially haunted locations in the dead of night?"

"Last time was during the day," I said, closing the car door and walking towards the Cineplex. I stopped and smirked. "Don't you come here all the time in the middle of the night to watch movies? What, now you're scared?"

"I'm worried you're not."

"I haven't been here in ages."

"Don't play the nostalgia card. It's not going to work on me. I am not particularly eager to relive my teenage years."

I started walking towards the door and Faiz followed. "I heard that this place used to be a skate park," I said. "Then they tore it down. Which is why all these kids skate in the parking lot here now."

"I know," he said, stopping. "I told you that."

We looked at each other for a second, before we said, "Always cite your sources," in unison and laughed.

I opened the door and motioned for him to go in.

It was busier than we thought it would be at 10:31 pm on a Thursday night. But people were bustling around, picking up tickets, buying snacks. There were as many people leaving as entering. They had those electronic ticket kiosks installed, and I could almost hear my dad talking about analogue formats for buying tickets.

"Why are there so many people here?" Faiz asked.

I shrugged. "Midnight showing?" I said.

"Yeah, but those have been going on all day. You used to only be able to see a new release at midnight the day of release. Now you can see them at 2:00 pm the day before." He paused. "When's the last time you went to see a movie, Laana?"

"You mean not on my laptop?" I asked.

"I meant not just a book."

"I don't read that much. That was a strange rumour spread around about me in middle school."

"I meant all your ghost research or whatever you want to call it."

Faiz pulled out his cinema pass. I rolled my eyes. Faiz grinned. "Now you have to ask yourself how much it's worth," he said. "For maybe a very slim chance of catching a glimpse of what may or may not be a ghost." I stared at the different movies being shown, scanning for the cheapest option, which turned out to be one of those independent, *Blair Witch*-style horror movies, while Faiz continued. "And even if you're right, even if it's true that you have actually seen a ghost..." He paused for what I assume was dramatic effect. "It may not be the ghost you want."

I tapped the screen and then waited a moment before taking out my credit card. "I've been thinking about that a lot," I said. "All the other ghosts on the blog. We'll never know if what we know about them is true, and what's false. We'll never know their stories. We don't know who they were, the lives they led. All those memories lost to rumours and relays."

"And just plain old forgetting," Faiz said.

The tickets practically jumped out of the machine.

"What theatre is it?" I asked.

"Thirteen," he said. "Just kidding. There is no thirteen. It was eleven, I think."

"Shame," I said. "I'd appreciate something being what it's supposed to be. But I'll settle for easy-to-find."

I hurried past the concession stand. I could almost see the fourteen- and fifteen-year-old versions of our friends huddled to the side, talking too loudly and laughing under our breath in order to seem cooler.

"Wait a sec," Faiz said. "I wanna buy some Sour Patch Kids."

"Are you kidding me?"

"You always need snacks for a stakeout."

"But this isn't a stakeout."

"Don't worry, the ghost isn't going anywhere."

He ran off to the counter. I didn't want to be alone with the shadow of younger me. I felt unsettled, a mix of dread, regret and embarrassment. I knew that if I kept remembering, if the memories materialised further, if I let myself find and put back together the details buried somewhere in my mind, I would piece together a story I would immediately want to forget. So I stood there trying to stop the cogs from doing their best to churn out a flashback, to reproduce and reconstruct a moment. I waited, trapped in time in between moments, not quite in the past, not in the present, but feeling it all at once. Not letting myself remember, but not fully able to forget.

Faiz came back, chewing the candy. He held out the bag. I shook my head. He shrugged, then looked at my face.

"You okay?" he asked.

"Yeah," I said, not looking at him, but staring off into the corner.

"You remember what happened."

"I'm trying very hard not to."

"I knew it would come up sooner or later."

I didn't say anything.

"We should talk about it at some point."

"Nope."

I started walking towards Screen Eleven. There wasn't a movie playing.

"Perfect," I said softly. I pulled the door handle. It was locked.

Faiz shook his head condescendingly. "What, did you really think it was going to be that easy?"

"Why is it locked? The Cineplex is still open for another four hours and what's there for anyone to steal? The chairs are bolted to the floor."

"Right, because people are so desperate for chairs."

I kept tugging.

"Mission over, let's go," he said, turning around and taking a step.

I grabbed the hood of his jacket. "Not so fast."

"Laana, you never give up," he groaned.

"I'll take that as a compliment."

I scanned around, then I saw an usher locking Screen Ten. I ran up to him. He looked familiar, but I couldn't quite place him.

"Hey, how have you been?" I said.

"Good," he said. He studied my face for a minute, almost as if he was searching for something. It looked like he couldn't quite place me either. "Haven't seen you around for a while."

"Yeah, I moved to the city," I said. "Listen, could you let us into that theatre?"

He looked at me sceptically. "Why?" he asked slowly.

"I, uh… left my phone in there."

"The cleaning crew would have handed it over if they saw it. You can check back here in a few days to see if anything's turned up."

"Please?" I said. "I can't wait a few days. I literally can't go home without it. I need it to call an Uber."

He looked at Faiz. "Out of battery," Faiz said quickly at the same time I said, "He's broke."

He surveyed us both, with even more scepticism than before. "Look, you know me," I said. "I went to soccer camp with your sister. In the second grade." I guess sometimes it pays to be from a small town where everyone knows each other – as long as he doesn't ask me her name. "I'll be really quick."

"Five minutes," he said.

"Thank you! You're a lifesaver!" I said as he unlocked the door. He handed me his flashlight.

"Oh, right, thanks," I said. All I had to do was remember to not take out my phone.

We ran in, our footsteps echoing in the silent room. I stood in front of the rows of seats and gestured to Faiz to take the lower half while I went to the upper. When we were younger, these rooms resembled those old theatres with fake boxes and red velvet curtains. They'd renovated them several times since. Now it was more modern, with large comfy chairs where you could press a button to recline the seat. The walls were bare. The screen was definitely bigger. There were fewer seats. This was no place for a ghost. It was blank, no history. But still, I swung the flashlight around. I stood, silent, trying to hear something, hoping to see something, anything in the theatre that would suggest a ghost had been there.

I clicked off my flashlight, just about giving up, and turned around to walk back to the doors. I hadn't seen Faiz reappear at my side silently and I bumped right into him.

"Did I scare you?" he asked.

"No, you're in my way."

He looked disappointed.

★ ★ ★

I hear a line and it reminds me of something someone said to me years ago, folding the page, creasing the spine, reaching back through time, collapsing it. There is no time anymore. It wasn't linear to begin with.

How can I ever be free from the past, when it keeps reaching out and pulling me back? When everything reminds me of something that happened years ago? When everything already happened before, and all events and decisions are repetitions of what happened to someone else? I am just living the same things over and over again.

Maybe we're all just trapped in circles, in loops, in the swing of a pendulum. Maybe we move away from ourselves only to return. We change only to snap right back into place. We keep returning to the same places. Maybe there's a limit to who or what we can be. There are all these detours, but only one destination. Any attempts at time travel only reinforce the existing narrative. Every option leads right back to the same outcome. The worst choose-your-own-adventure: there's only one ending.

★ ★ ★

Sometimes you know the ways things are going to go. You know what decisions you are going to make. Not out of predetermination, but out of habit. You know what you're going to do because you've always done it, always thought about doing it, never thought about doing anything else.

So, when Amara asked me to hang out, I said yes. It was a thing I still did at that point. But she mentioned Faiz was coming, and it had been over a year since the Halloween incident, which was the beginning of the end of Sairah and Faiz's friendship. But things changed in tenth grade. By then, not only had Sairah and Faiz stopped talking to each other, barely anyone talked to Sairah anymore. She had only mentioned him twice since Halloween – both times to say he lied and had falsely blamed her for things she hadn't done, like cheating on her test. Our friendship group would have effectively been splintered if it were not for the fact that Amara and I were still close, and Devon and Jay were cousins. Other than that, it was me, Sairah and Devon on one side and Amara, Jay and Faiz on the other.

(Amara, Jay and Faiz don't speak anymore. A mix of growing up, growing apart, having been too close at the wrong age.)

But I went that night. I told Sairah I was watching a movie with my parents. A sort of half-lie. I was, in fact, watching a movie, I told myself. It wasn't as bad as if I told her I was doing something else, I rationalised. Now, I think, it doesn't matter in the way lots of details lose their sharpness, their sting, over time, but only I would argue with myself over details.

After the movie, we were hanging out and talking. "It's good to see you, Laana," Jay said. "You never hang out anymore. Not without that freak Sairah."

Jay was flicking a lighter open and shut.

"You started the rumour," Devon said.

"Haven't you wondered why everyone was so quick to believe it was Sairah?" Jay responded. "She's so weird. Nobody likes an outcast. They had all turned on her long before."

"Let's go," Devon said, grabbing me by the arm. But I wasn't going to say anything. I wouldn't, in fact, say anything for ages.

In the years afterwards I wouldn't remember what was said, all I would remember is that I didn't say anything. I didn't defend my best friend. I never once said anything nice about her in front of others, never pushed or fought back. I consoled myself with the fact that I wasn't concerned with my social standing, but that I just didn't want to deal with the fight. Once again, I was too tired, too lazy, or maybe too complacent, too unwilling to do the right thing.

★ ★ ★

If time really was cyclical, what did it mean that we just kept coming back to the same place? That we were either stuck in a loop or trapped in a town? Could physical distance ever equate to temporal distance? Did progress sometimes mean how far you got, literally? All our fates tied inextricably to this one small town, a tiny pinprick on a map, an even smaller mark in the vast stretch of history, a brief, miniscule, insignificant flash in the grand scheme of things.

I know that time can stretch and bunch up and it can collapse, but it's always running away from me. It's like trying to keep up with a train as it pulls out of the station, knowing I should have been on it. I never have enough time for anything. I always need more.

Chapter 8

This is a story I tell myself: my parents would give me these elaborate Lego sets to play with while they graded papers, and that's why I wanted to be an architect, and that's how I got interested in buildings, which led to me getting one degree, and then signing up to do another in art history. This thing happened when I was a kid, and so this is why I am the way I am. But it's just a story. Lots of kids like Legos. They also gave me books and stuffed animals (I did want to be a vet for a while, despite never being around real animals – I never had a pet and Clifton never had a zoo). There were so many paths. There were contributing factors but there were also things that didn't make an impact, no ripples. When you're going through it, you look for signs, some way to predict an outcome. And afterwards, you think you know what led to what. But it's a simplified account, in a familiar shape, a reverse pattern where you know the ending, and so you can rearrange what came before it, building your own narrative.

* * *

From *Clifton: A History*, page 136:

> *The Haywards, who took special care and pride in the appearance of their house and surrounding land, would open their compound to visitors as a public garden from time to time. Gardening was Annabelle Hayward's special interest, and she spent a lot of time making sure the gardens*

were in good shape and inviting people over to see. The grounds remained open to visitors after the death of Carolyn Hayward, as stipulated in her will.

★ ★ ★

"How did you know I would love Lego sets so much?" I asked.

"That wasn't from us," my mother said. "It wasn't even our idea. Your Daadi gave that to you. And, like everything else, you played with it for a month and then lost interest."

"Except for Play-Doh," Dad said, looking up from his papers. "You loved Play-Doh."

"I loved Legos," I said.

"You did," Mom said. "You loved lots of things. Then you moved on. I guess you just forgot about it."

★ ★ ★

From *Carolyn Hayward: A Life*, chapter titled "Carolyn at the Hospital":

Carolyn Hayward was well-liked by her patients, especially women and younger ones. In letters, her patients and their parents pointed out how good-natured she was, her kindness, her sense of humour, but mostly how they felt she took their concerns seriously, took time to understand their problems, and made sure they understood her insights and advice.

★ ★ ★

"How's the research going?" Mom asked, startling me. She had asked softly, not in her teacher voice, and I hadn't heard her come in.

"Mystery solved: it was tuberculosis. She didn't die a violent death."

"Weird, huh, how we all believed it? How we almost expected a woman would die that way?"

"I hadn't really thought about it like that."

"I think we're too used to it."

"Because we have to be."

She nodded. "But I'm glad you questioned it. Would be terrible if you spent all that time with us and at school and it turned out you were a terrible researcher."

I laughed. I once looked my parents up on one of those professor-review websites, just to see what their students thought of them, and almost every one of my mom's reviews pointed out she had a good sense of humour. Most people found her hilarious, except one person who said they wished she'd stop making such bad jokes. But that was the thing about Mom, she couldn't help herself, she had to make every joke regardless of quality. She wasn't scared of anything, certainly not a bad joke.

"I did find something interesting," I said. "Some of her patients wrote short letters. They said she was really kind, always making people smile and cracking jokes."

"You don't know how happy it makes me to know that the 150-year-old ghost and I would have gotten along," she said, totally deadpan.

★ ★ ★

I loved the days where I could research any random thing that came to mind. The summers when I could have gotten ahead on my studies, but didn't really have to so instead I spent hours looking up filmographies of up-and-coming actors, watching video essays about overlooked indie films, searching for fragments of unreleased albums, reading about an internet theory that an influencer had secretly ghostwritten a very popular series of crime novels. Each little thing I could find that would lead me to something more, something bigger, all these holes to travel down, not fall, but float through and discover, one tiny point splitting out into an infinite number of paths that kept branching on and on forever.

★ ★ ★

"Is your answer to every problem to do extensive research?" Faiz asked, as I was flipping through tabs and tabs of reviews for a movie that had just come out that day.

I didn't look up.

"Laana, why art history?" Faiz tried again.

"Look who's asking a lot of questions for once," I said.

"I thought you wanted to be a scientist like your mom," Faiz said.

Sairah and I looked at each other and laughed. "Laana can barely add single digits," Sairah said.

"It's true," I added. "I keep mixing up years and messing up how old Carolyn was. I couldn't tell you when she was born or died or how old she was when she finished nursing school."

"This is a great story, though," Sairah said.

"Right, so, I was running late —" I started before Sairah cut me off.

"As usual."

"But this time I overslept," I said. "I rarely oversleep. So, I'm late, I run to the campus coffee shop to get coffee because there's no time to get food, I barely make it to class on time. But, in all the chaos, I had looked at the wrong day on the schedule and ended up in the wrong class in the wrong classroom. It was already too late by the time I realised. I was on the other side of campus. There was no point in trying to make it to the other class. And the class I was in was —"

"Art history," Sairah finished.

"And the syllabus was so interesting that I didn't want to leave," I continued. "The class I was supposed to be in was biology or something, so you know I already failed. I knew I wasn't good enough at the math part to become an architect and also

I wasn't willing to put the extra year in. So, I stuck with art history."

"And now you read about old stuff and... buildings all day?" Faiz asked slowly.

"I like it," I said. "I'm good at it."

"At least you know that."

★ ★ ★

Two people could be talking about me, but they're not talking about the exact same person. Sometimes other peoples' impressions of you are stuck in a certain moment of time. Like how your relatives have all these stories of when you were a little kid, but don't remember that you switched your major, or when your parents can't remember that you no longer watch crime shows. Or an old friend sends you a meme that you don't find funny, that vaguely references a hobby of yours that you lost interest in years ago, and you hope this means you've grown, but really it means they didn't know you that well to begin with.

★ ★ ★

I try to read another biography of Carolyn, but I can't focus for memories. Every place has its counterpart, every name its descendant, every detail has its parallel; it reaches up from the book and back into my mind, connecting the facts of her life to memories of my past, hazy overall, but surprisingly vivid in moments.

It's not always memories or movie-style flashbacks. Sometimes it's just facts that pop back into my mind at random. A statement, a sentence. I suddenly remember something I hadn't thought of in years. It's insignificant, inconsequential. It's not relevant to anything else, there's no context. Pieces, fragments of a larger story. I can't remember all the details. Just a single truth. I don't know what's around it.

There's no narrative, no constellation to be made by connecting the dots. They're not stars, they're just points on a graph, not a map with clues. Uninterpreted, raw data.

I used to think these memories were trying to tell me something about my past or my present. I thought they were giving me the chance to reevaluate and understand my past as my present self, knowing what I know now. Or I thought they were a reminder that time is a lake, life is an accordion, we're not really going anywhere, just retracing our steps, skating in figure eights. Or maybe they're just there to remind us we have a past, we're still the same person we were then even if we know more now, that we can't put distance between us and the past.

★ ★ ★

"Nostalgia's a trap," Taylor said. "Everyone hates high school."

"I don't," I said. "It was okay. It wasn't bad. Middle school, on the other hand..."

She raised her eyebrows. "But you wouldn't want to go through it again."

"Oh yeah, definitely. It wasn't that much fun either."

"Nobody wants to relive anything. Everyone wants something new."

"Yet you sell loads of old records."

"Nostalgia does sell."

"But it's different with history. I get it. It's like this is the best we have. Things have never been better for us."

"And still they suck."

"People who look like me didn't come to this town until, like, forty or fifty years ago. The country my parents are from wasn't a country a hundred years ago."

"I don't want to know what it was like for my ancestors. To go back in time would be catastrophic. People need to stop romanticising the past."

"I do love a good period drama."

"You wouldn't survive a period drama."
"A lot of people didn't. We have TB shots now."

* * *

From *Three Families of Clifton: A History of the Emersons, Haywards, and Norcotts*, page 225:

> *Like other women of her social class in that time period, Carolyn wasn't expected to get a higher education or to work. But after reading a book about nursing schools, she enrolled at the Connecticut College of Nursing at the age of twenty-one. She performed well and graduated at the top of her class a year later. She returned home to Clifton right after graduation and immediately started working in the maternity ward at her family's hospital.*

* * *

People misinterpret you all the time, misremember, misunderstand you. You're a different person to everyone, whether you notice it or not.

People have ideas about you that aren't entirely true, and you won't always be around to correct them. To be fair, everyone you know, and even some people you don't, walk around with ideas about you in their heads, but you can fix them, or at least try, but you'll never know exactly what they think about you, and they'll never know you, exactly, wholly, entirely.

And to some extent, you don't want them to. You don't want someone to pin you down with frightening accuracy, because it gives them an advantage: they know you better than you know them, almost as well as you know yourself. And I think a lot of people think they've got others figured out, because they want to give themselves the advantage. A kind of narcissism, or laziness, convenient thinking: flatten others because it's easier, you don't have the time or energy, or because it didn't occur to you that they were more complex than you thought, that there were things you didn't know. Or because maybe you know you'll never have all the pieces, so you just have to work with what you have. You don't leave the gaps open because you don't want them there and you don't want to think about how you can't fill them.

The sad thing is there's always more to learn, more pieces to find, collect, fit and build, more gaps to fill and more gaps to discover. And you won't get to do that with some people. They'll remain mysteries, constellations, unfinished jigsaws, lost to you forever.

★ ★ ★

From *Centuries of Clifton*, page seventy-three:

> *Carolyn Hayward enrolled at the New England College of Nursing at sixteen years old and graduated at the age of twenty-one. She was second in her class. She worked at a hospital in Boston for six months before moving back to Clifton and working at Hayward Hospital.*

★ ★ ★

Years ago, Sairah became obsessed with things like tarot cards and fortune telling and signs and omens. I thought it was funny. I'd heard our moms talking about how children grow into their nicknames, so they tried calling us things like "early bird" and "helper" instead of "sleepyhead" and "dozy" – the latter being Sairah's nickname because she often zoned out. Later we found out it was because she was actually too advanced for most of the classes she was in. We never grew into these nicknames, sleeping in too late and getting distracted by our phones and forgetting to keep on top of our chores. But Sairah started reading things around us. This is a sign you'll make the team. This is a sign you'll get into this college. This is a sign this is the career you're meant to have. And I wanted those things so badly that I began to believe her, believing I could will things into existence just through wanting them. That I had cracked some key to the universe that let me know what was happening. That I could read the code. That I knew what was going to happen.

But it wasn't fortune telling. It was wanting, wishing, worrying, a desperate grasp for reassurance. Confirmation bias, which was confirmed when neither of us got into the colleges we wanted to go to.

The thing that interests me is all the supposed signs I missed. The art classes I took when I was younger. My mother playing in the cemetery. My dad at Carolyn's house.

Or the irony. Applying to the university I actually ended up going to on a whim just before the deadline. Faiz claiming he saw a ghost all those years ago, only to be back hunting for a real ghost with the same people he tried to prank. Sairah was destined to become this good at baking, even if it's just because she procrastinates the writing she feels is her true talent.

I looked around at my room. All the signs of who I would become were here. All the things I tried to fight for so long. All the things I thought were detours were destinations. It was inevitable I would end up the person I am, obsessed with history and second-hand records and old things, wanting to stay inside and read and research and think. Not really needing the outside world when I could think of what was and what could have been. I was always going to find Carolyn.

I used to think these were all phases, distractions. Now it seems foolish I didn't see that it was always meant to end up this way. I was always meant to end up here.

But if I had always known how it was going to end, would I have done anything differently?

★ ★ ★

"How're things at Taylor's?" Sairah said.

I looked at her puzzled. I hadn't mentioned it to her.

Sairah laughed. "You practically lived there in high school. I didn't think you would come back without a few visits there."

"I've been helping out."

She nodded. "I guess it keeps your mind off things – well, the one thing you don't want to talk about. You can change the subject now."

"How did you know I was going to change the subject?"

Sairah shrugged.

"I didn't even know."

* * *

Sairah and I spent the day taking personality tests. To our surprise, Sairah had changed two letters on the Myers-Briggs. Mine was identical. The same it had been when I took it in college and high school.

"Have I changed?" I asked Sairah. "I used to think I had, but now I'm back I'm just reminded of all the ways I've stayed the same."

"It's this town," Sairah said. "Nothing's changed. It makes you feel like you're trapped."

"It's the same with you," I said. "It's just Clifton that's making you feel this way."

"I actually am stuck and I did it all by myself, thank you very much."

"Yeah, well, believe me. Moving somewhere else doesn't make you feel any more mature. But I get what you mean; this place is a time capsule."

"I don't know that anything really changes. You know what I'm talking about Laana, we're still dealing with all the same issues we were dealing with ten, fifty, one hundred years ago. The same issues Carolyn had to deal with are probably not that different from what we face now."

My problems had just evolved from what they were when I was younger. The same problem just kept coming back, each time in a totally new and unrecognisable way. I don't know how long I'm supposed to stay trapped inside the same circle.

★ ★ ★

From *Take Care: The Story of Nursing in Twelve Women*, "Chapter Eight: Carolyn Hayward":

> *Carolyn Hayward never went to nursing school. At the age of eighteen she started working in the maternity ward of Hayward Hospital.*

★ ★ ★

"Do you remember that book I was writing in the tenth grade?"

I thought for a minute. I remembered one summer where Sairah got really into going to coffee shops and sitting for hours and hours, presumably writing. I was supposed to be doing some sort of work, I think maybe my college essay, but I was scrolling through Tumblr. But Sairah was actually writing. She told me about the book as she worked on it, and it changed throughout the summer. It started out as a story about a young girl who ran away from home. Initially, the novel was about the road trip she went on, but later Sairah got more interested in writing about a missing girl from the perspective of her family. I think at one point it was a murder mystery, at one point she faked her death.

"About the girl who went missing?"

"I still haven't finished it."

"Writing books takes a long time. I'm sure many successful writers have spent years and years writing their books. It also seemed pretty involved. What's it been, like six years?"

"It's been ten, Laana. Ten."

"Some things take longer," I shrugged. "It'll pay off, though. It'll be really good."

"I'm stuck. I'm paralysed by either insecurity or ineptitude and either way I'm starting to think it's time to call it quits."

"You're just going to... stop writing? You? Really?"

Sairah sighed and nodded.

"After all this time, you're just going to walk away?"

"I've put in enough time. Nothing happened."

"That doesn't mean it won't happen."

"I'm going nowhere, Laana."

"But you've always wanted this. It's who you are."

"People change."

"Don't you think you owe it to yourself to keep trying? You can't just pour all that time down the drain."

"Just because you've invested in something doesn't mean you need to stick with it. Sometimes it's good to know when to cut your losses."

"So, what will you do?"

"Find something that requires less time, less emotional involvement, less investment."

★ ★ ★

It was raining on the first day of first grade. We were both late and met while taking our rainboots off in front of the classroom – we were wearing the exact same pair. The rain had caused the street next to Sairah's to flood, which meant a bunch of the roads were closed and Sairah's mom had to take a longer route to school.

My parents and I didn't have much of an excuse – we were always running late. It was genetic. I was late on the first day of school every year. And most days after that.

So, we were late that morning. My parents were unbothered about being late. I think they found it funny that they spent all their time dealing with precise numbers and complex equations, yet couldn't arrive to a single place on time. I think they ended up accepting it as an inevitability, even then. I have a memory of that morning before I met Sairah: my mom pulling my purple-and-yellow sweater over my head, my old brightly coloured building blocks scattered around me. My dad sticking his head in from the kitchen, fastening a tie. "We're ten minutes behind schedule," he laughed. "We'll never make it on time now." My mom smiled at us and said,

"Well, we never were going to, were we?"

It was a new school for both of us. I had gone to a separate kindergarten closer to the university and Sairah had gone to the Montessori past the hospital. Since we were both late, we ended up sitting in the back row of the classroom, alone together and, at that age, that can make a whole friendship.

I've always thought that if it wasn't raining, we wouldn't be friends. Sairah wouldn't have been late, we wouldn't have met at that moment, we wouldn't be wearing matching rainboots, we wouldn't have sat together. I've asked Sairah about it and she thinks it was inevitable. We're so similar in so many ways, she thinks we would have gravitated towards each other naturally. She thinks the shoes were a sign we had a lot in common; the fact we picked the same pair showed we were somehow connected.

I thought the rain was fate.

★ ★ ★

"Do you ever feel like life is just so short?" I asked, as Sairah scooped batter into the muffin tin. "Not that I want to live forever, just that there are so many things I want to do, and you only get one life. It's not even a time thing, it's a possibilities thing."

Sairah was licking the batter off the spatula, lifting up her shoulders and flashing a quick smile as if she was caught doing something she shouldn't. "I get it, it's like when you apply to college and it's exciting, and then you hear back from colleges and it's even more exciting getting your acceptances, and then you have to choose and it's so disappointing because before you had all these paths and now you have one."

"Exactly. It's like you could have been a completely different person or led a completely different life if you had picked a different school. But I also think about all of the jobs I could do, like I could teach elementary school or be a college professor or do research or be a journalist or work in a museum. They're not all that different – they all involve similar skills and knowledge – but they're all completely different paths. And I can't decide."

"And I chose to stay here," she said.

"That's not so bad," I said.

Sairah seemed distracted by something on the counter. She scrubbed at it with her finger, first lightly, then harder. "Huh," she said, peering at it. "Has that always been there?" I looked. There was a piece of glass embedded in the granite countertop. It sparkled and glowed turquoise, out of place. "Can't believe I never noticed," she said.

"I have a scar on the back of my hand," I said. "I have no idea how it got there." It's not like the scars on my knees, which I assume were from falling off my bike. I really don't know what happened. I have no recollection of getting it. "You'd think I'd remember that. It's funny because people always say they know things like the back of their hand."

★ ★ ★

Sairah organises her bookshelves by colour. She always has. Even the notebooks she writes in. Those were colour-coded by time. Every few years, she'd switch colours. She explained this to me soon after making me promise to burn them all, set every colour of the rainbow on fire until they were all the same shade of deep charred black. She pointed out the blue notebooks from elementary school, the black-and-white composition books from middle school, then the slim red leather ones from high school.

"My juvenilia," she said, her fingertip running along the lengths of their crimson spines.

"Your what?" I giggled, sounding younger than sixteen, which I was at the time.

"Juvenilia," Sairah said, in that matter-of-fact way she used a lot as a teenager.

I swallowed back my laugh and tried to nod maturely, like I understood. Sairah could tell I didn't.

"It's what a writer wrote when they were young," she explained.

"How young?" I asked.

She shrugged. "I don't know. I guess it depends. It's like trying to figure out when you're grown up."

Her juvenilia ended junior year, when she took a hiatus from writing to focus on college applications, before starting up again with purple notebooks in college, and green afterwards. I bought her an orange one when I came back on this trip, certain it wasn't a colour she had. It was on the shelf, an identical one lying on her bed. Two extra notebooks. My first thought was that I was going to need more lighter fluid. My second was that I couldn't bear to watch all her hard work burn. I had always known that when it came down to it, I wouldn't have the heart to destroy what was left of my best friend. I don't think I'd ever do it. I guess that makes me selfish.

★ ★ ★

"How's the book going?" I asked tentatively. I could have said a number of things. I wanted to stop her from stopping.

"I don't think it's ready," Sairah said. "I don't think it'll ever be ready. I've sunk so much time into trying to salvage it, but I don't know what to do with it. No one will take this if I submit it now, and if I show it to people – editors, publishers – I'm afraid they'll remember it the next time I try to show them something and won't read it. I don't want this to be the first thing anyone reads from me. I just don't want this to be..." she trailed off.

"Your legacy?"

She nodded.

"Yeah, that's a scary thing."

"And it's a book, Laana, it's a whole book. Once I put it out there, it's always going to be there. It'll never go away."

"And it'll belong to other people. And they'll all look at it in a different way."

"And they'll all look at me in a different way."

"Yeah, well, just don't go reading the reviews." I took a sip of my coffee. "You don't get to control what other people think of you," I said, as much to myself as to her.

"Otherwise we would have had more friends in high school," Sairah laughed.

"Yeah, I was too busy scaring them off with my questions."

"And me with my poetry."

"I liked the one about the spiders."

"Yeah, you were the only one."

"Do you think you're also scared of showing people exactly who you are?"

"Oh, that's what I'm most afraid of. That this is all I am. That I publish it and it's bad. It's the perfect representation of my talents. It's the best I can do, and it's not good enough. Or that there's something in there I didn't realise I put in, something about myself, and someone else figures it out and sees right through me and they know actually I'm a bad person."

"I'm scared of being a bad person too." I didn't tell her I was already starting to realise I was.

Chapter 7.5

But there was a fire. Not at the time of Carolyn's death, or during her life, but in ninth grade. At roughly 7:47 pm on a Friday in April – Maghrib time, sky was a milky blue-grey – a custodian locking up the school saw flames coming from a patch of trees in the woods behind the school. It was a small fire, put out quickly. There was no damage, no one was hurt.

I was staying at Amara's house and we were at the cemetery when the fire started. I remember the sun setting behind the fences, burning its brightest right before it started to fade, the warm glow dripping with regret. Then the cool chill dragged over the graveyard, the coming dark turning the greens and greys blue. I sat there and thought about how sad it felt to watch the day end with all the graves surrounding us, feeling like something much bigger was ending, some rare opportunity had just passed us by and now something much sadder was going to happen. And, in a way, I was right. I knew somehow. We went to see a movie after that, so we had an alibi. There was no way we could have made it across town in time for the 8:00 pm showing if we had started the fire. It was a terrible movie, and we had to hold on to the tickets for evidence. I still have mine in a shoebox somewhere. Amara and I avoided the cemetery for weeks after that. Amara thought it was bad luck. I didn't want to get so close to getting caught again.

Sairah was at home, reading. Hena was sleeping over at a friend's house. Their parents were out to dinner. Devon had cancelled on Sairah to hang out with the debate team after rehearsals. For weeks afterwards, Devon would say that they never should have cancelled. If they hadn't, Sairah would have had an excuse. I never pointed out that they could have just asked Sairah to come along. Because I could have done the same thing.

Jay, Faiz, and a third person – a friend of theirs whose name I could not remember – all played basketball together on Fridays after school. But Jay's brother, who was at home, covered for them and said they were playing video games at Jay's house. Nobody had any reason to question it. I later found out from Amara that the boys were known to hang out in the woods in the evenings.

That unfortunately left Sairah. She was never officially accused because there was no evidence. No one knew how the fire started. Sairah couldn't provide an answer because she hadn't done it. But that didn't stop people from talking. All we had were rumours: matches, a lighter, blowtorch, witchcraft. An art project gone wrong, a hex gone right, an accident, ill intent, revenge. Hena pleaded that it was a natural brush fire, or maybe some electrical malfunction. Sairah said over and over again that it wasn't her, that she was at home. But no one believed her.

A bad reputation is worse than doing something bad. According to others, Sairah fit both cases. She was weird and dangerous. An outcast, a teen girl in a horror movie. Even her parents stopped getting invited to people's houses. Hena had a hard time making friends, one time yelling at Sairah for costing her her social life. She knew her sister didn't start the fire, but she blamed her for not making more of an effort to fit in. By being on the outside, Sairah made it more believable that she was the perpetrator. Hena had a much better time once Sairah went to college, and so did Sairah.

Some months after the fire and the rumours had been extinguished, Sairah and I were sitting in the garden at her house when I asked her, "How did the fire start?" I had always assumed it had been an accident. She was my friend and she would have stayed that way, even if she had done it on purpose. But the rumours had gotten to me. I thought she was behind it.

She looked at me, her eyes angry behind the rapidly filling tears, "How could you not believe me?" she said, before running into the house and shutting the sliding door so quickly it shook back and forth, offering a brief glimpse of her before she disappeared to her room.

Her mom saw what happened and told me she'd be okay and, maybe because she was like a mother to me, maybe because she looked like a version of Sairah from thirty years into the future – a version who was calmer and happier and had got through this difficult period in her life, who probably didn't remember it, maybe even laughed at it – I believed her and listened to her. She called my mom to pick me up.

Sairah was quiet the next day at school. A few days later, things were back to normal between us. I did believe her at that point. We never spoke of it again, not ever, not even when I saw Jay flick the lighter open at the movie theatre.

★ ★ ★

It was one of those big, flat rectangular ones. There were cartoonish flames drawn on the side, but the rest was gleaming silver. I still remember it, throwing flashes of light around the dark red walls of the lobby, so bright I could see them now.

Devon eyed the lighter. "It was you," they said.

Jay laughed and put the lighter in his pocket. "What are you talking about?" he shrugged, showing us his empty palms.

"You told everyone it was Sairah," they said.

"That," he said, flicking his eyes quickly towards Faiz, "wasn't my idea."

"You have to tell everyone the truth," they said. "You started the rumour. And you started the fire."

Jay laughed again. "Why would I?"

"You needed to point the finger away from you, but why'd you have to point it at her?"

"Haven't you wondered why everyone was so quick to

believe it was her?"

"If you don't tell them, I will."

"No one's going to believe you."

Jay was right.

★ ★ ★

After the night at the movies, Devon tried telling everyone it was Jay. But nobody could believe that Jay, whose family had been here before Clifton was Clifton, who was part-Hayward as well, who had more in common with a ghost than most of the town's residents including the girl he blamed for the fire, could have done anything to damage the beloved hometown his great-great-grandfathers had made.

Most of this was true for Devon as well, since their family had also been one of the first families in Clifton. Devon's accusations were baseless, people said – but so were the accusations against Sairah. Jay's parents had covered for all of them, and Jay's parents owned a lot of the buildings in the town, including the building leased by the restaurant Sairah's parents were having dinner at.

I still hung out with Jay and Faiz. I still speak to them, and I told myself it was only to get to the bottom of it, but that was a lie. And I never really did get to the bottom of it. Initially, the boys threw around "campfire," but they stopped once they realised there wasn't much reason teenage boys would go camping right behind their school. In the times since, I've tried to ask Jay, "Do you still have that lighter? Where did you get it? What did you need it for?", but he wouldn't say a word. Faiz has maintained "science project" when questioned.

Some people were scared of Sairah, and me by association, which I kind of liked. I wasn't intimidating by nature. Even when I got into arguments in classes it was seen as a brief annoyance or momentary flash of anger. Sairah, on the other hand, was confident and defiant, and I saw people cave during class debates later in high school, as if in fear that her steady, focused glare alone – eyes narrowed, gazing deeply, eerily calm instead of volatile, more like a laser than the unpredictability of flames – could set them alight. In comparison, I was a spark that couldn't catch, an ember that faded and disappeared.

Sairah stayed who she always was, keeping to herself, reading and writing lots. It came in handy that her favourite hobbies were solitary ones – not just ones you could do on your own, but ones that were best done in quiet and isolation. Her curse was that she couldn't leave Clifton. Despite doing well academically, she couldn't get into most of the universities that would have taken her across the country, even across oceans, and the ones she did get into were too expensive. Faiz ended up going to Berkeley – Sairah's first choice – his final victory in what started out as a petty academic rivalry and turned into an all-out contest. She said to me several times that he didn't deserve it. The university – the one my parents worked at, barely an hour from our house – offered Sairah a scholarship. She didn't want to take it, but it was too good to pass up. It was easier to live at home, so she did. When she got her first copywriting job straight out of college, it was remote, and couldn't cover rent in any big city. At some point she had stopped trying to get out.

Chapter 9

Years ago, in that introductory art history class I stumbled into, we learned about pentimento – when in an artwork you can see signs of something that has been painted over. Outside the examples they showed us in class, projected in an auditorium with a hundred other people, I never found any, but I searched for them every time I went to a museum. I kept trying. I looked for them in the stories I heard, in the books I read. Some evidence of who Carolyn was hidden beneath the layers, some fact in the fiction. Or even a slight flicker which showed how the stories came to being, when and how they changed.

The word comes from *pentirsi*, which, in Italian, means repent.

★ ★ ★

I mentally shuffled around blocks in my calendar, clearing up room, days, weekends. I blocked out time for travel. I asked for days off work. I didn't go on a trip with my friends. For once in my life, I made the train on time. I made the trip home. I spent the weekend, whole weekends, and I made time and I put in effort. And I realised, yes, I could have found a way, things could have been different.

But you can't change what happened. Because in the end, and all the times before that, I wasn't there.

★ ★ ★

"I feel like I've been playing the longest, most unhinged game of broken telephone ever," I said.

Sairah laughed.

"Just running around, asking people, 'Have you heard about Carolyn?' Then I had to add books and old newspaper clippings to it."

"But you're getting somewhere," Sairah said.

"Am I? Or am I just getting further from the truth? The funniest part of that game was how outrageous and different the phrase became by the end."

"I feel like everyone made it weirder on purpose."

"What was even the point of that game?"

"To get children to whisper instead of yelling. And to sit all in one place for a little while."

"I thought it was to teach people that things get lost when you relay information through people. You have to go straight to the source."

"Now we know why you liked it so much." She started walking. "Honestly, I don't think they were trying to teach us good research practices. I think the message is not to spread rumours or trust them."

"Whatever the purpose, it didn't work. Rumours are how we got all these Carolyn stories."

"We got these Carolyn stories because people like to embellish and sensationalise and aestheticise and exaggerate death and make it horrific and terrifying."

"Maybe that's why people came up with her story in the first place," I smiled. "They wanted some excitement around here."

"That makes the most sense to me, especially since she didn't do anything bad. It's just good, old-fashioned woman-hating."

"Yeah, it's either: become a scary ghost or be burned at the stake."

"I bet you those women were good at science or something. And people thought they were doing evil magic."

I nodded. "That makes sense to me."

"Have you tried asking Ms. Mirza?" Sairah asked. "Maybe she would know."

"She taught world history, though," I said.

"I'm sure she knows loads about local history. Her family's been here for centuries."

"What?"

"Her last name before she got married was Emerson. They got here before the Haywards did."

We walked for a few moments in silence before I managed to take a deep breath. "I saw the lighter," I said. "First semester sophomore year. I was at the movies with Faiz, Jay, Amara and Devon, behind your back. And Jay was playing with the lighter. The same lighter he used. He did it."

"So that's why Devon was so convinced it was Jay," Sairah said with a small smile.

"I'm so sorry, I should have believed you," I said.

"Yeah, you should have," she said. I should have known she wasn't going to let me off easy. "You were my best friend. I gave you no reason not to believe me."

"They were my friends too. I guess I believed them."

"This is what I mean. You knew how they treated me. I would tell you and you didn't take it seriously. Even now, you brush it aside like it was some childhood thing, inviting Faiz to hang out. At first I thought you were trying to fix things."

"I really wish I could." And I wish that had been my intention.

"But then I realised you actually didn't remember."

Not remembering isn't the same as not caring, I wanted to say. "I didn't," I admitted.

"They told everyone it was me. I was almost certain they had done it, covering their tracks. When Devon told me, I was so happy. But no one believed them either. And you, you've kept it to yourself all these years."

I didn't say anything. What could I say? I didn't have an excuse.

"Everyone blamed me for years, and for years I've had to deal with them whispering, cancelling on me, turning the other way. And it would have been so much easier if I had known you believed me, but you didn't."

"I'm sorry."

"You can't go back in time and fix it," she said. "But you can do something about it now. You can be there for me now."

★ ★ ★

How do we know we were supposed to end up here? How do we know we weren't supposed to end up somewhere else, that there wasn't a glitch in the system? Maybe we're in the detour. Maybe we've veered so far off path that we've reset everyone else's fates. Maybe we got lost and had to course correct.

When I was younger, I liked the idea that everything was supposed to end up a certain way, that there was a fixed chain of events, a predetermined outcome, a static fate. If you believe that it was all predetermined, that it's out of your control, that things were meant to go a certain way, then you can't mess up, you can't go too far off course, you can't irreparably change things.

Then we started growing older, and those fates started unfolding, and the pieces started falling into place, and most of us were unhappy with the outcome it was leading to. This couldn't be what was in store for us, could it? And if it wasn't, then where did we go wrong?

How fixed was that fate, and what would it take to change it? Was one person, one decision, enough to throw it all out of balance? There's a ripple effect, a chain of events, a line of dominoes, a butterfly in a hurricane. Was it possible to mess up so badly that you ruined everything? Could I have doomed myself and everyone else?

★ ★ ★

Walking into school was the weirdest part of the trip home. I felt like I had unlocked a whole new set of memories that I wanted to shut away in a box and fling into the ocean. I just had to keep the lid on the box long enough to have a conversation and to not shudder visibly every five minutes.

The campus was bigger than I thought it was. I'd gotten used to the idea that everything in our small town was tiny.

The classroom looked different, but then it did every year I was at school too. Mirza was good at changing things up. I never asked her if she liked decorating. I also later found out that teachers often paid for their classroom decorations out of their own pocket. I never thanked her either.

We sat on a bench overlooking the soccer field.

"Do you know much about the Haywards, especially Carolyn?" I asked.

"If I remember correctly, you didn't seem to like local history," Ms. Mirza said.

"Yeah, I think I asked to have it cut from the syllabus in our end-of-year evaluation," I admitted.

"Can I ask why the sudden interest now?"

"I – uh…" I tried to come up with a good excuse, or to brush it off. I ended up with, "I saw that Hayward Manor was scheduled for demolition."

"It's been scheduled for demolition for years. They just haven't gotten around to it. Who knows if they ever will."

"I'm just surprised nobody pushed back against the demolition. I thought it was a historic landmark or something."

"This town is constantly changing. It'll change again. I think a lot of people don't see any reason in holding on to the history of something that feels so far away, so different."

"Were the Haywards really important to Clifton? I know about the hospital of course, but did they do anything else important?"

"I think they may have helped with funding for City Hall and what's now the library, possibly even this school. I guess their influence runs deep."

"And Carolyn?"

"Dedicated nurse. That's pretty much all I know about her. Weird, isn't it? All I know about her is her job."

"Rare for a woman in that time."

"I wonder if she really was a workaholic."

"She must have been lonely. Do you know anything about how she died?"

"That's always been the question. I couldn't tell you. Everything is equally plausible to me, but I've heard so many different versions I don't believe any of them." She paused. "You know, I had a student years ago who was really interested in this stuff. Did a whole project – you know the secondary sources project, you did one too – on the Haywards. She does a lot of local history research now. Maybe you should talk to her. I'll see if I have her email."

★ ★ ★

While taking a break from my research, I decided to crack open one of my mom's books. It was a collection of horror stories, ordered from least to most terrifying. I remember my mom saying the book wasn't actually that frightening, but she said that about everything, even horror films she went to the movie theatre to see by herself because my dad and I were too scared. The first story was titled "Memento Mori", which I'd heard before, but I didn't know what it meant. I looked it up. Memento mori – a symbol kept as a reminder of death. Isn't everything a reminder of death? Your medication, an EpiPen, an inhaler, a whistle, a phone, a flashlight, a lighter. Don't we prepare for everything? Isn't everything a reminder of death when death is the opposite of life and everything is part of life? Don't we always think of the worst-case scenarios? Aren't we constantly thinking about our own deaths, but only briefly, walking up to the ledge and looking, then quickly snapping our heads back and walking away? Instead of really looking down at what's below.

★ ★ ★

Thankfully, Dr Alyssa Wang was an adjunct at the university. I met her at the campus bookstore's coffee shop.

"Thanks for coming here to meet me," she said.

"Thank you for taking the time to meet with me," I looked around. "I haven't been here in years." I looked at her. "My parents teach at the university. I came here all the time as a kid."

"Oh, what department? Do you think I might know them?"

"Math and engineering. I didn't get either of those genes."

"But you're an academic. You're getting your PhD?"

"In art history."

"Do you want to teach?"

"I just… want to do research."

"I get to do loads of research. I only teach once a week."

"That's actually what I wanted to talk to you about."

"Oh yes," she pulled out a booklet. It was bound in those little curved combs, with a clear sheet of plastic on top. "My thesis on the Haywards." Then she pulled out an even larger stack of paper. "I actually did way more research, enough for a book, but I couldn't find anyone interested in it enough to publish it."

"Was all this on the Haywards?"

"It had to do with the development of healthcare in the region. I study history of science. The Haywards had more to do with it than most people realise. They ran the hospital and let a woman take over, who did a better job of caring for women and children than most other hospitals in the area. Then they all followed them."

"This is great," I said, picking it all up and staring at it. "Thank you."

"Can I just ask how you became interested in the Haywards?"

I thought for a second. "I think it's for the same reason you research anything – you want to get to the bottom of it, to piece together who they were, what they did, why we still talk about them today. Even if it is only to tell a completely made-up ghost story."

"Yeah, it seems like everyone missed the point."

"But you didn't."

"And neither did you."

"Wish there were more of us. And that there was more interest in your work."

She shrugged. "Occupational hazard. The ghost story is more interesting, I guess."

"Oh, it's not nearly as interesting as the truth."

★ ★ ★

I was alone again in the house, reading Alyssa's research:

> *Although for generations the town of Clifton has been obsessed with speculating about how Carolyn Hayward died, it is almost certain that she died of one of a number of diseases or illnesses. Hospital records indicate that around the time of Carolyn's death, several patients were admitted with cases of chickenpox. Southern Connecticut had a high incidence of scarlet fever and tuberculosis at the time. Carolyn's diary entries contained references to symptoms consistent with a range of illnesses: fever, cough, chills, fatigue. Hospital logs show that she had taken the day prior to her death off sick.*

I saw movement outside the window. For a brief moment, I thought maybe it was her, that maybe all of the warnings about somehow summoning her had been true, that I had done the research, the leg work, the hypothesis, and now I would be rewarded with a glimpse, proof, even if no one believed me. Maybe I wouldn't get an answer, but I would experience it, somehow get closer to her than I could from all the books, even if it was a brief apparition, a flash of smoke.

I got up from the couch and looked outside. It was a deer, staring back at me, scared. I was envious. I wish I had been scared.

★ ★ ★

There are stories about loves that survive death, and sadness that is passed down from generation to generation. But what about anger, frustration, guilt, regret, fear that lasts longer than you do? Because I am filled with so much guilt it feels like this body, this lifetime, cannot contain it.

Chapter 10

It was the third time I pushed back the trip. I didn't even have to buy the train tickets in advance. I told everyone that I had to work. I thought I could go next weekend, or the weekend after. I don't know why I didn't go then. None of the reasons make any sense now.

I came the day before the funeral. I was supposed to come the day before, actually a few days before, actually a week before, actually there wasn't supposed to be a funeral. Actually, I was supposed to come and visit my grandmother. And I didn't. I wasn't there.

It would have been better if I had a reason. If there had been a meeting, or a job interview, or something I could not have gotten out of. If I had a doctor's appointment, or a friend I hadn't seen in years was coming to the city for the first time in ages. Or maybe if I had made some terrible and unexpected mistake, if I had overslept or my hereditary knack for always being ten minutes late had kicked in and I missed the train, or, better yet, if the trains were cancelled, if there was track maintenance, a freak storm. If fate or some forces – any force – greater than me had intervened.

But no, it was all me.

And without any reason. It was just me, by myself, who cancelled the trip, because – and back then I couldn't explain it, and now I can't justify it – for some reason I just didn't want to. And then I didn't.

★ ★ ★

On the train ride home I thought about whether, if time travel were possible, I would go back in time and un-cancel the trip, knowing what I know now. My immediate, knee-jerk reaction, as soon as I found out, was to regret not going. I regretted everything, I regretted not being with my parents, not getting there soon enough, not getting to see her one last time, not being there when it happened, having to hear it on the phone.

I don't think wishing you did something differently knowing the outcome is the same as regret, I think it's just acting on better information. I think it's just normal.

And that's just one trip. What about the others? What about the years spent away? What about all the people and their problems I ignored?

I don't think there's an option that eases the regret.

★ ★ ★

I made it in time for the memorial service. It was a blur. I couldn't tell you what the weather was like. I don't even remember what I wore. All I remember was Sairah and I lying side by side on top of my bed, feet still on the ground.

"Sorry I didn't send you a card," Sairah said. "Or buy you flowers. Or get you anything. It felt weirdly performative."

"It's all performative," I said. "Us sitting here not saying anything feels the closest to anything real."

"I figured showing up was better than a card."

"Oh, totally. It was a good excuse to get away from some of the visitors."

"Sorry we couldn't hang out under better circumstances."

"I'm sorry, too."

More silence. Except we could hear my parents talking to other parents downstairs.

"This is what grief really feels like, emptiness," I said to no one in particular.

That, and the fact I didn't shed a single tear the whole day.

★ ★ ★

Weeks later, I was consumed with thoughts about how I should have grieved. How I should have acted, not with the cool, concise, matter-of-fact statements I always talked in, jumping abruptly from topic to topic, getting distracted, spending most of the time with Sairah. I wish I had stirred up some emotion. Even a little anger would have been out of the ordinary, surprising. It might seem a little unusual, but understandable. Normally, people prefer sadness, but if not, they'll settle for rage. Calmness, though equally justifiable and likely, starts to feel unusual, almost suspicious.

It would have been better if I acted with my mother's graciousness and gratefulness, pleasantly surprised at any kindness offered to her. It would even have been better if I had been weeping, tearful, visibly shaken like my father, the tissue in his hand and the cracks in his voice evidence that he was grieving, that he felt.

But I just stood there, quiet and cold. Not really there, because I hadn't been there when it mattered.

And that's all I could think of. That's why I couldn't correct my behaviour, didn't think to perform. All I thought about was what I would have needed to do to make the trip. I calculated ticket prices, was so busy trying to recall train times that I forgot to help my mom in the kitchen. While people tried to offer condolences or make small talk about my degree, I thought about what I was working on that week, how no paper could possibly be worth this, that some small delay or even a big one wouldn't have mattered, not in the way things matter now. That things would never matter in the same way again.

★ ★ ★

"What's it like?" I asked. "Working for your dad?"

"Oh, you know," Faiz shrugged.

"I don't know," I said.

"Right, because you turned into your dad instead," he said.

"No, I didn't," I said, affronted.

"You're an academic. Like your parents."

"But they teach. I don't want to become a professor. Also, their subjects are so different from mine."

"Different shades. Same paint."

"You didn't answer my question."

"It's fine. Dad gives me loads of bonuses," he said with a smile.

"I'm sure logistics isn't the most interesting thing," I said.

"It's definitely not what I thought I'd be doing. Or where I thought I'd be doing it."

"Are a lot of people moving out?"

"Enough."

"Is anyone moving here?"

"Some."

"Is it hard to watch all those people leave Clifton for good, when you had to come back?"

He was staring out the window. "You have no idea."

★ ★ ★

The truth is, I was turning into my dad. In a sense, I am my mother and my father. I actually look like it – you'd think I'd be exactly half and half. I am less like my mother than I thought I'd be. I don't have her patience or her selflessness or her ability to see people and communicate with them on their level. I'm more like my dad, asking questions, laser-focused on a task, picky about music, stubborn.

I like research. I'm bad at math. I get so sucked into work I forget to eat lunch. I like the city; my parents prefer the suburbs. They never left Clifton. I hated coming back.

★ ★ ★

"Do you remember Adriana Navarro? Who I worked with on that book?" Sairah asked.

Sairah had, in the course of her various attempts to make a living by writing, at one point been a ghostwriter. She had worked with a bunch of other ghostwriters, including Adriana, to write an autobiography for a once-mildly-famous photographer. Sairah, who spent so much time thinking about what writing would be associated with her name, had only been published under someone else's name. Her name essentially erased.

"So, she worked on the screenplay for *Raincheck*, but she couldn't get credit for it because it's a hard process. I actually don't know much about it. But then she wrote her own screenplay and no one would take it."

"What were they about? The screenplays?"

"The one she wrote herself was about women during the Salem Witch Trials. The other one, the one that actually got made into a movie, was some slasher film. Anyway, she was telling me all the stuff she found out about the witch trials. She said she wanted to focus on what life for women was like at the time, not just –"

"How they died," I completed. "Please don't tell me you're trying to tell me something here."

"Yeah, that I only befriend people with the same weirdly specific interest. I told her about your research, and Carolyn, and obviously she was interested. So, if you have anything that's readable, you can give it to me and I'll send it to her."

"I should compile it, make it presentable. I think a lot of people would be interested, or should be. You know, everyone's gotten it all wrong. But none of it's readable right now. It's all Post-its and Notes app entries and photos and random scraps of paper and scribbles in my notebook –"

"Same notebook you've always carried around," she said with a smile.

"I wonder where I got the idea from."

★ ★ ★

"Laana, why did you call me that day?" Faiz asked.

I stopped and turned around.

"Was it because of Sairah?" he asked.

"Honestly, it's because I saw you in the supermarket," I said. I wanted to tell him it wasn't that deep, it was random, chance, he was one of a few faces I saw and recognised and wanted to say more than one-word sentences to. I didn't want to tell him that I remember so little, that half the time he or Sairah mention someone we went to school with I have no recollection of them, entire lives wiped from my brain. How one time Sairah showed me a photo of someone I had a class with and it was a total stranger. I could not place her or remember her name or her voice – it was like I had never met her. I didn't tell anyone that for the past few weeks I had been haunted by the face of a former classmate whose name I could not remember for the life of me. I remembered her face, that was it. I didn't even know how I knew her. I had forgotten huge chunks of my childhood, pieces of my own history lost to time. Fragments of my past, of me, missing.

"I wasn't thinking about anything that happened with Sairah," I said. I didn't say I didn't remember or had forgotten. It seemed kinder, like I hadn't ignored what they went through.

"We were just kids," he said.

"I know," I gave a slight smile. "It feels like a long time to hold that against someone. Sairah doesn't." I didn't know if that was true. I didn't realise all they were holding on to.

And I didn't explain the overwhelming guilt that had been creeping over me for the past few weeks as I pieced together what happened and what I had done, or, more importantly, what I hadn't done then, and what I didn't do once I realised.

"Do you remember that book you gave me?" I asked. "About those weird turning points in history?"

He nodded.

"It was a surprisingly thoughtful gift. I never told you that. It was a good choice."

"You and Sairah just wanted books. You still do. It makes things simpler."

"You're a good friend. Maybe a better friend than me."

"That's not true."

"Those turning points – no one would have acted that way if they had known things were going to end up like they did. It's only ironic when you look back at it. When you go through it, you just think it's another decision."

He let out a hollow laugh. "I wouldn't use the word 'ironic'."

"Neither would I," I said. 'Tragic' was what I would say. But again, I didn't.

"You were right, it's not always a good idea to go back," I said, worried that if I actually did have the chance to go back in time, to do things over again, I still would have been too scared to act, that I would have made the same decisions all over again, that I was still the same person, doomed to repeat the same mistakes, unable to escape regret or the worst parts of myself.

★ ★ ★

It was becoming more and more surprising to see who people grow into, like some twist ending to a season of a TV show. You hear stories about where they are now, like some non sequitur to the person you used to know. You don't know if it's the outcome that throws you off, or how they got there. You wonder if secretly they were like that all along. If they had some grand scheme that made the pieces fit together too well. You think back to any warning signs you might have missed. Or, instead, you imagine scenarios, try to figure out what twist of fate led them down this path. The hard part is figuring out which person was the real person: the one you knew or the person they became. Had they wandered down the wrong road or just finally course corrected?

Sometimes the people you could predict are the ones that surprise you most. The kid in your class who always said she wanted to be a doctor shocks you by getting into medical school. You get used to the uncertainty. You think things never work out exactly like you want.

"I don't know if I believe in fate," Sairah once said. "If I think too hard about it, I don't feel like doing anything."

Why do all our words dealing with a fixed outcome sound like fatal?

★ ★ ★

"What's Amara up to these days?" Sairah asked.

"I'm not sure. I think she's still working in finance. I barely talk to her anymore."

"Oh really?"

"I spoke to her when I got here, but that was the first time in a while."

"You guys were always so close," Sairah said.

"Yeah, she's one of my oldest friends. And our parents were close so, you know, we were always at each other's houses. Basically, when I wasn't with you, I was with her."

"That's what I thought. What changed?"

"I guess it happened in college. We grew apart. Or maybe in high school. We had different interests."

"Yeah, must have been hard for her to keep up. Yours were always changing. Like when we kept taking up instruments, but instead of bothering to practice we'd just switch to another one."

"Remember our fake band?"

"I cannot recall the name. It's right there, but it won't fully materialise in my brain."

"Weird how we never grew apart."

"It's not that weird. We just influenced each other so much we basically became the same person."

"But it's weird that that happened with you and not with Amara."

"I mean, it's not like I knew her that well to begin with, but when I see her photos online, I feel like she's a whole different person."

"Is that more surprising or less surprising? That she grew into a different person, and we didn't?"

"I know you're supposed to change, and it's normal and encouraged and everything, but it shocks me when there are people we know who changed so much."

"But at the same time, is that who they were supposed to be all along?"

"Which one is the real you? The one you used to be? Or the one you became?"

"I guess they both are. But we remember the old Amara. We don't even know her now."

It's like they aren't even the same person. It's like the current version doesn't exist. It's like we lost her.

When someone you know moves away, or exits your life in a less finite, mortal sense, you sometimes mourn them, grieve the loss of your friendship. That's how final that feels. I think it's harder to accept you've grown apart from someone than to pretend that they're still in there somewhere.

★ ★ ★

"Writing is a fairly recent invention in human history," Sairah said. "We've been talking and telling stories for so long, but not writing them down as much. That's why oral histories are so important."

"Someone should tell that to our tenth-grade history teacher," I said.

"We did, I believe. There's so little local history about us here in Clifton. We were left out of the history books."

"We do have oral histories," I laughed. "If all the stories our parents tell about living here and us as kids count."

"I always felt like most of those were exaggerated."

"Maybe this is our history," I said, after a pause.

"A ghost story?" Sairah asked. "Which you've proved is mostly false?"

"Not the ghost story, the story of the story. How we all talk about a nurse who's been dead for years. Everyone growing up in Clifton for generations – even though the town changed a whole lot – has heard the stories of her. It's like a shared reference, an inside joke –"

"A folktale," Sairah finished. "This is how stories and myths and legends happen."

"All those stories had an agenda. Some countries' origin stories were myths and legends that were told and changed and written and rewritten."

"And what happened to those countries?"

"They may have tried to take over most of the other countries and succeeded for a number of years, which has had catastrophic consequences for us even today."

"They took over the countries our parents are from."

"What an inheritance."

"We're not writing history."

"Fine, but we're doing something, we're a part of something and we're a part of this town and its history and how it gets remembered."

"Let's just hope we're in the history books years from now, when our grandkids go to school."

"Everything written about us is about culture and family and generational issues. Well, we have ghost stories and ambitions and fears and big creepy houses and graveyards too."

Sairah smiled. "It is a good story."

"She was an impressive ghost," I said. "And an even better nurse."

★ ★ ★

We're told that you should have a clear narrative. Your college essays, your job applications, people you meet expect you to fit a neat description. Events in your life should build to something which connects to the thing you want. To sell yourself, you need to have a good story. You feel the need to squeeze yourself into a particular shape and shed what doesn't fit. You feel conflicted over the parts of you that don't support that narrative. You start to buy into it as well.

Maybe we're not stories or narratives, but just a collection of statements, of facts, some more true at some times than others. We're just random observations, the quotes we put beneath our Instagram posts, the details we choose to include in our Twitter bios, the bullet points on our résumés. The standout memory a college friend has of you. How your friends introduce you to your other friends. The ideas others have of you and the ways you try to control and pre-empt those narratives.

There would be no need to try to force it into one whole, one identity, if we weren't constantly being asked to define, to describe, to present, to construct a narrative, to tell a story, to introduce ourselves, if we weren't so afraid of uncertainty. We weren't really supposed to combine it, weren't meant to make sense of it.

And this is what is lost, the fact that there never was supposed to be a whole. That you can get to an answer, that there is a truth, but you will never fill in all the blanks, store a complete person in your head. That didn't, couldn't, shouldn't stop me from trying.

★ ★ ★

"For what it's worth," I said. "I don't think you're a failure."

"Thanks," Sairah smiled. "And I don't think you're a weird, ghost-obsessed history nerd."

"Who's saying that?"

"No one... apart from me."

I laughed. "At least you know me well enough."

She looked at me, confused. "Of course I do. We've known each other since the first grade."

"I feel like maybe I don't know you as well as you know me. I can't tell if it's difficult, or if I didn't try hard enough. I had no idea what you were going through."

"I didn't want you or anyone to know. If anything, I'm glad I was able to keep it from everyone. I don't want your pity."

"You just want to feel unstuck."

"See? You got it," she nudged me. "Not everyone is some mystery for you to figure out."

"But everyone kind of is. You don't really know what you're going to do or what you're going to be like or even if the decision you're making is the best for you."

Neither of us said anything for a while.

"I just have to say this. I'm sorry. For not believing you about the fire, for not saying anything, for not thinking about what you went through. I don't care if you forgive me or not —"

"I forgive you."

She caught me off-guard. I didn't know what to say. I wasn't expecting that.

"You can forgive yourself now."

I laughed.

"I know you, Laana. You didn't think I would forgive you because you haven't yet. And you won't for a while. Take your time. Just know that this is no longer on me."

Chapter 11

"How come I never get to pick where we hang out?" Faiz said, lagging behind us as we walked through the park.

"Okay, you pick next time," Sairah said, stopping and turning to face him as he caught up. "Where would you go?"

He faltered and looked around. "Um, here? The bridge."

"Interesting choice," Sairah said. "Why the bridge? Is it because it's conveniently in your line of sight?"

"Or because there are ghosts there?" I said, joining them. "Oh, right, you don't believe in ghosts."

"I've indulged your ghost obsession," he said. "Maybe you guys should indulge my love of structural engineering."

"I didn't know you were an engineering enthusiast," I said.

"Well, you would if you were paying attention to your very alive friends instead of reading about some nurse who died years ago," he said. "And now trying to find her instead of doing normal people things."

"If you're too scared, we don't have to go," I said.

"I just want to pick at some point," Faiz muttered.

Sairah shrugged and started walking again.

"All of these wild goose chases," he said.

"This isn't one of those," I said. "The thing we're going to see will be there. It's always there. They literally can't move."

Faiz grimaced. "How much farther?"

"I didn't know he was going to whine so much," Sairah said to me, but loud enough that Faiz could hear it too. "You must have driven your parents crazy on road trips as a kid."

"It's real close," I said. "Exercise is good for you."

"I miss my bike," he said.

"What happened to it?" I turned to look at him.

He shrugged. "I stopped riding it. My mom got rid of it at a yard sale."

"Ah, yard sales," Sairah said. "The great erasers of time."

"Didn't know you were this sentimental," I said.

"I didn't know you were either," Sairah said.

"Guys, can we call an Uber or something?" Faiz said. Sairah and I just kept walking, faster this time, while Faiz yelled after us and half-jogged to catch up.

We reached the edge of the park and crossed the street, leaving Brooks' Books behind us. We walked past Hayward Manor, the gates looking as if they would outlast time itself. We travelled a few more blocks, walked by Devon's parents' house, which had been in their family for generations but where the youngest generation no longer lived, and the apartment building where our middle school humanities teacher used to live.

"We're here," Sairah said.

We had reached the gates to the cemetery. Tall and black. Grand in the broad daylight. Empty, except for all the graves and the bodies under them, and the souls that may or may not have remained.

Faiz didn't say a word as we walked in. Sairah started pointing out where the people in our history books were, a natural tour guide despite her handful of visits. I didn't even know this much. I didn't think to connect them to the books or brochures, I just ran past them, faces in a crowd, names I didn't have lives to connect to. Sairah went on to talk about some people we sort of knew, relatives and ancestors of acquaintances.

"Where do you think you'll be buried?" Sairah turned to ask me.

"Oh, good question. I wonder if my family has a plot or something," I said. "I guess it would be cool to be buried here, you know, after all the time I've spent here." My gaze briefly, involuntarily, darted over to the one part of the cemetery I always tried, and failed, to avoid. "On the other hand, I just want to be put into the ground, no coffin, no grave, no nothing, and just disintegrate. So, I guess it doesn't matter where."

Faiz looked horrified. He still hadn't said a word since we got to the graveyard.

"I also kind of like the idea of nobody knowing where I'm buried. Like I could just be buried in some random woods somewhere," I said. "Completely anonymous."

"How am I supposed to visit and leave you presents?" Sairah said, mock-outraged.

"What makes you so certain you're going to outlive me?" I said with a smirk.

Faiz wandered over to a row of graves. It was a family who had died in the early 1900s. Eleanor, James and Marie Ashford. He poked the grass at the foot of the graves with the tip of his shoe.

"Are you gonna be buried here?" I asked Sairah.

She laughed. "Of course. I'll never leave Clifton. My body will be stuck here forever."

"If you never make it out of here, you could send your body to be buried somewhere else," I said. "Would be kind of interesting. Being buried someplace you've never been."

"Yeah, it would be cool to do things in death that I couldn't do in life," Sairah said. Again, my eyes flicked over to that spot. I shook my head, clearing my vision.

"I know I'm looking forward to that," I said. "To finally be free of this flesh prison." I wandered to a bench and sat down.

Sairah walked over and joined me. We waited for Faiz. He stood there, looked around for a bit, then came over.

"So," I asked tentatively. "What do you think?"

He took a deep breath. "It feels… so strange. And, I don't know, like an entirely different place."

"Otherworldly," Sairah interjected.

He glared at her in defiance. "I guess you could say that. It's like all the normal stuff we talk about and think about doesn't really matter."

"Wow," I said. "You're starting to sound like me." Sairah and I laughed. "The cemetery has changed you, bro."

"I just don't understand how you can joke and laugh and act so carefree when we're literally surrounded by hundreds of dead people."

"Oh, good question, Laan," Sairah said, turning to me. "I wonder how many people are buried here. I'm sure there's a way to find that out."

"Doesn't it, I don't know, make you feel something, to be surrounded by all of this −" he gestured, waving in the air as if sifting through it for the words.

"Maybe for you, but not for Laana," Sairah said. "She comes here all the time. This is literally a walk in the park for her. I guess this is a park. It is very green."

"But it does," I said softly. "The knowledge that there is a concrete, finite ending and the comfort that whatever is bothering me today won't be a problem forever."

"But how can you be so calm, faced with the fact that we're going to die someday? That we'll be gone, and all that will be left is a slab in the ground, if that. Doesn't that scare you?" Faiz asked.

"I think about death all the time," I said. "It doesn't scare me."

"Is it death that scares you?" Sairah looked at Faiz. "Or not being remembered?" she said, mock-intellectually.

"Or is it fear itself?" I said, and we laughed.

Faiz just stared at us, baffled.

"I just think it's interesting," Sairah said. "Women aren't supposed to worry about death, we're historically supposed to be concerned about giving life − even though not every woman can or chooses to. So, what? We're just supposed to not be scared?"

"My mother has no fear," I said. "Watches horror movies all the time. Never seen her so much as flinch at a jump scare."

"This isn't a horror movie, Laana," Faiz said. "This is actual death."

"We're meant to die as soon as we're born," I said. "It's as much a part of life as breathing or talking to other people or sleeping."

"What does scare you, Laana?" Faiz asked. "You have to be scared of something. No offense, but I don't think you're fearless."

"I don't know," I said, glancing out at the gravestones.

"Being wrong?" Sairah asked, leaning towards me.

I dismissed her with a face and a wave. "I guess being a bad person. Or maybe not being as good a person as I thought."

"I thought you were going to say failure," Faiz said. "Or being forgotten. Or remembered wrongly." He turned to Sairah. "What about you?"

"Oh no, this isn't some first-day-of-the-semester icebreaker," Sairah said. "We're not going around the circle and saying what our deepest fears are."

"It's not an icebreaker, it's a guessing game," I said. I pointed at Faiz. "Death." Then I pointed at Sairah, "Failure. Easy."

"You know it's not that easy," Sairah said.

"You're right. You're also scared of not being able to control what happens to you and your work in other people's minds."

"Are you more scared of not being understood or truly being seen?" Faiz asked.

"You're catching on!" I said. "See, cemeteries put everything in perspective. How can you be worried about some awkward text you sent someone when these people have to deal with these epitaphs forever?"

"What awkward text?" Sairah asked.

"Nothing," I answered, maybe a beat too quickly. "I was speaking hypothetically."

"Sure you were," she said.

"Okay, Faiz, you ready to see Carolyn?"

"I hope you mean her grave and not her body or her ghost," he said. "Either way, I'm going to regret this."

We walked up the hill. Well, Sairah and I tried to take it at a sprint while singing loudly and Faiz trudged silently behind us.

We stopped. The air was cold, and I could see my breath as

I panted. I had been here too long. I hadn't been here enough. My hood was up over my head. I pointed at the collection of marble-white tombs, graves and statues. We walked to Carolyn's statue and stared at her in silence for a little bit. At eight feet, she was the tallest structure in the cemetery, apart from the mausoleum at the other end, and much taller than she must have been in real life. She had long, straight hair, but most of it was covered by a hood. The statue had a long, plain dress. Her features weren't sharp, but small and smooth. She reminded me a bit of cartoon Carolyn from one of the books my mom got me from the library when I was younger.

"That's it?" Faiz said. "She could be anyone."

"It's funny, isn't it?" I said. "This isn't a representation of who she was, but of who we remember her as – some mythic, larger-than-life figure, watching over all of us." No defining features, other than the fact she was gone.

"Do you think she knew?" Faiz said. "That we would keep talking about her for hundreds of years after she died."

"No," Sairah said.

"I don't think she cared," I smiled. "I think she just wanted to save the lives in front of her. I don't think she had time to think about what would happen after she died." I knew she thought about and faced death all the time, but I wondered if she thought about her own death.

"It must be really annoying to have a permanent statue that looks nothing like you," Faiz said.

"Or stories," I said. "Everyone tells these stories about you that have nothing to do with who you really were."

"She must hate the fact that we talk about her," Sairah said. "And the fact we talk about her as this scary, horrifying presence terrorising people."

"Who knows, maybe there will be another ghost story in a couple of years and it will be one of us," I said.

"Oh my God, please don't tell me that's your long-term goal," Faiz said.

"I don't think or plan that far ahead," I said. "Besides, I hate people telling stories about me."

"I'll do it," Sairah said. "I'll gladly take that responsibility. I'll be the Ghost of Clifton future. I always knew I would be more famous after I die. If I'm stuck in this town forever, might as well make the most of it. I haven't done much with my life."

"That's not true," I said. "Besides, we need you to tell the ghost stories. Or, I guess, come up with them, and the variations."

"As long as I die in an interesting enough way, we won't need any of that," Sairah said.

"People are pretty creative on their own, without even realising," I said.

"Watch out, Faiz, it would be a shame if the residents of this town in a hundred years implicated you in my murder," Sairah said.

"I wouldn't blame them," he said. "It sounds like the ending I deserve."

★ ★ ★

I've just been doing laps around the same person I was. Every time I changed, started to turn into someone else, I would double back, be the same person twice as hard, go even further in that direction. In high school, I thought I was going to suddenly become good at math or science, but I ended up getting sucked into history. In college, I wanted to major in something responsible and practical, like economics, but barely passed the intro-level class. Again, it was history. When college was almost over, I knew I should look for a job outside of academia, something different from my parents and what I had always known, and even managed to send off a few applications before starting a PhD.

I kept coming back. No matter how far or for how long I tried to stay away, I kept coming back home.

There is no static fate and there is no cohesive self, but it does feel sometimes like there's a person you're supposed to be, the person you are and the person you will be. And there's some overlap, less like a Venn diagram, more like a projection.

★ ★ ★

Sairah opened the door. "It's so good to see you all!" she said, mainly to my parents.

After they were inside, she said to me quietly, "Late, as usual."

I shrugged. "We can't help it. We were kind of made this way."

Hena wasn't there, so it was just me, Sairah and our parents. Other than Hena's absence, it felt like any other time we had had dinner with Sairah's family. We could have been in high school, or home from college. It was the first time we had been invited to dinner since I'd been back purely for socialising and not out of sympathy or to condole. I always thought our families were too close for that.

It had been two months. I wondered how I'd feel a year, two years, five years, ten years afterwards. I wondered if it was a sharp drop or steadily decreasing, like every day it hurt a little less, every day the same amount of tiny, incremental change.

Sairah was laughing with my mother. I guess we were always family. Maybe that's why she forgave me so easily, or rather seemed far less angry at me than I deserved. It's different with family. You're stuck with them, until you're not.

Dad asked her about work. "Oh, Laana, I've been meaning to tell you. I finished my manuscript draft," she said.

"That was fast."

"Yeah, well I had been working on it for the better part of a decade. I think it was almost done anyway. I just needed a little push to finish it."

"How long do you have left on your PhD?" Sairah's dad asked me.

"Two years," I said.

"Then you'll be a professor, just like your parents," he said.

"Well, not a professor, hopefully," I said.

"She had to rebel in some way," Dad said.

I came close to being like them then veered off, in the same way I only half-look like each parent.

"Our little researcher," Mom said.

"She is good at that," Sairah said.

"I could never do it," Mom said. "I loved the hands-on parts and field research, but sitting reading articles and books was the worst part. Writing reports? Excruciating. But Laana does it all without complaining."

"I think she prefers it," Sairah said.

★ ★ ★

Some people are remembered, some are celebrated. Some get resurrected through movies and articles. But then there are so many people who are just statistics, just names, just tombstones, not objects of affection. Victims, but not heroes or martyrs. Tertiary characters, not the protagonists. Images, examples, to make an argument. Plot points. Not the story themselves. There'll be no documentaries, there won't be discussions about who will play them in the film. They won't appear in the film, save for as part of a number in the title card at the end.

★ ★ ★

After dinner, I helped Sairah put away the dishes.

"You should come to the city with me," I said. "My room-mate's finishing her degree at the end of this semester. You could move in. Your work's remote anyway."

Sairah shrugged. "I don't know, cities are overrated."

"Too expensive?"

"It is an expense, and it's not necessary."

"It would be nice to get out of Clifton," I said. "Like you always wanted."

"I have a life here now."

"You want to stay? After everything they put you through?"

"Most of them don't remember anymore. Or they don't care. Some of them think it's funny, that a fifteen-year-old tried to burn down the school –"

"Allegedly," I interjected.

"Some of Hena's friends thought I was a hero by the time they finished high school."

"You forgive them?"

"I don't know if it's forgiveness or if I just got tired of holding on. I think eventually I just lost interest."

"But even before that you hated it here."

"It's grown on me."

"Really?"

"I think it's grown on you too."

★ ★ ★

Time is like a river. Time is like a lake. Time is like a tree trunk, adding rings with each year. Time is like the branches of trees, so many possibilities leading out. Time is linear. Time is concentric circles. Time is a flat circle. Time is happening all at once. Time is measured according to the sun. Time is measured according to the moon. Time is a construct. Time is in parallels, so our lives, the alternatives, the main narrative are in other dimensions.

None of it helps. None of it changes what happens. It doesn't help me change the past, I can't go back and take that trip, and even if I did, I don't know where I would end up and if that would be any better than where I am now. I can't stop people from believing it was Sairah, I can't make them un-believe it now. It doesn't give Faiz any extra time, or stop him from worrying he won't have enough, that he's running out.

There's only ever one ending, in the end. The same one each time.

Chapter 12

Sairah's backyard had this treehouse we used to play in all the time. We'd climb up there with our backpacks after school and read books. Sairah's mom was very particular about us keeping them up there. Our books are still there. It was huge and well-built, which meant both of us could still sit up there together. We didn't know who built it; it came with the house.

Sitting in the treehouse, memories came back to me of the games of Pictionary we played, all the scavenger hunts and treasure maps. I suddenly remembered class activities where we solved puzzles, mystery books I read in middle school, the forensics class I took in college. The time a friend hosted a murder mystery dinner party and yet it wasn't as scary as when Sairah and I stayed up late watching crime shows in high school. All the YouTube videos we sent each other about unsolved mysteries. The obsession with solving. Not the obsession with fear, of making your skin crawl like horror movies, but instead the joy of finding things out, the pride of piecing the puzzle together, the sense of achievement when you've solved something, the comfort that it can be solved, and most of all the feeling of being right.

Sairah's treehouse turned out to be big enough to hold the three of us and boxes of school projects we had found around our houses. We started exploring them while making our way through the bags of candy Faiz bought from the store. I was eating more than looking.

"Hey, do you guys remember this?" Faiz held up a letter. At the top it read: "To twenty-year-old me."

"I don't, at all," I said.

"Oh God, I don't want to see that," Sairah said. "And we're about four years too late."

I rummaged through my box and found mine. "Here it is," I said, holding it up.

Faiz and I turned to Sairah, who gave a big sigh and looked through her box. "Here we go," she said a few minutes later.

"When was this?" I asked.

"It must have been fifth grade," he said. "Who wants to go first?"

"This should be fun," I said.

"I don't want to go at all," Sairah said.

"I'll go first then," I said. I started reading: "'Dear Laana, I hope your life is going well'," I looked up. "Nice polite opening."

"You were already good at emails," Faiz laughed.

"I hope you have a dog by now, and lots of books," I looked up. "Well, I'm one for two there."

"Not bad," Faiz said.

I continued. "You're probably in vet school –"

"You wanted to be a vet?" Faiz said. "I didn't remember that."

"Yeah, I don't know how or why. Clearly, I was way off."

"You couldn't expect a kid to know they wanted to be a PhD candidate in art history," Sairah laughed.

"But I know you and Sairah are really close. I know you'll be friends forever." I looked at Sairah, who smiled back at me. "Another thing I got right. I am blessed with the gift of prophecy. 'Everyone tells me school is really hard, so I hope you do a good job and come home soon and that you get to take care of all kinds of animals.' I was either entirely accurate or completely off. You next," I nodded at Faiz.

"Dear Old Faiz." He stopped. "I hate young me already. 'A lot can change in ten years –'"

"Wise beyond your years," I laughed.

"As always," Sairah said.

"Ha ha," Faiz mocked. "But if I'm right, you're probably in astronaut camp."

"Boy, you really set yourself up for failure there," I giggled.

"Laana, when have you ever come in close contact with an animal, like, ever?" Faiz said. I stopped laughing. He kept reading. "You're going to be the first astronaut to visit Pluto, the smallest planet —"

"No longer a planet," Sairah interjected.

"Thank you, Dr Awan, I don't see you going to astronaut school anytime soon," Faiz said.

"Astronaut camp," Sairah giggled.

"Honestly, you two are never going to let me finish," he said, then continued. "Or maybe you'll get to visit a moon or an asteroid. Anywhere's better than Clifton. But you probably have flying cars now so it's easier to get to other cities. Anyway, I hope astronaut school is more fun than regular school and I hope you can afford a flying car."

"I like how ten-year-old you was really sober to the realities of finances," Sairah said.

Faiz shrugged with a smirk.

"It's weird how we thought technology was going to progress faster," I said.

"Yeah, now all we have are apps that aren't really good for anything other than sucking up all our time and knowing us better than we know ourselves," Faiz said.

"You wanted to get out of Clifton," Sairah said.

"Yeah, didn't we all?" Faiz said. "Only one of us succeeded."

"And it's the one who sits in the library all day," Sairah said. "Which you could do anywhere."

"I think we're missing the point here — we all thought we would be better at science than we are," I said. "I thought you wanted to be a movie director?"

"Filmmaker," Faiz corrected.

"Oh please," Sairah muttered. Then we looked at each other for a split second and burst out laughing.

"I did, but later," Faiz said. "Like in middle school."

"Do you still want to?" I asked.

Faiz nodded. "I mean, I have no idea how to do it or how it works, but I love watching movies. I'd love to be a part of them myself."

"Sairah could write you a script!" I said.

"Laana!" Sairah protested.

"Okay, sorry. I promise not to volunteer other people," I said. "After this. It's your turn, Sairah."

Sairah lifted up her letter. She took a deep breath. "Dear Future Sairah, I'm sure by now you're on your tenth book – I'm on my first now. I hope London's nice and you have a big sunny apartment filled with cats."

"I'm sorry, your dream was to become a cat lady?" Faiz laughed.

"That's what you got from it?" Sairah said, not annoyed but genuinely curious.

He continued laughing. "Yeah, it's just, like, dream bigger."

"She did," I said. "Ten-year-old Sairah had loads of plans for books."

"I used to write a lot faster than I do now," Sairah said.

"That's not a surprise," Faiz said. "Everyone knew you were going to be a writer. Books take ages. A ten-year-old wouldn't know that."

"Another thing a ten-year-old doesn't understand is that you can't afford an apartment in London solely through writing – which made me slower at writing because I had to get another job," Sairah said.

"So, what we've learned is that the education system has failed us when it comes to economics and science," I said.

"And education. Apparently, I thought I was going to be out of college by twenty?" Sairah said.

"It seems ten-year-old you had an… unusual understanding of time," I said.

"Or you didn't plan on going to college," Faiz said.

"'You're probably a super-famous writer and you've already won the Newbery' – I didn't know about writing awards for adults yet — 'And I hope you're really happy because you have the best job ever'."

"You were right about that," I said. "You've always loved writing."

"Is that what you were worried about?" Faiz asked. "That you haven't done any of those things?"

Sairah looked down.

"You were the only one who was right," Faiz said. "You're the only one who still is who they thought they would be. And you were completely confident. None of this 'I hope you still like this when you're older' stuff."

"Is it satisfying to actually be who you wanted to be?" I asked.

"Laana!" Faiz said.

"I don't know," Sairah said. "It feels disappointing, knowing how it's going to go and there not being a twist or a surprise. Like when you watch a movie and it's exactly like the book it's based on, word for word. I said I was going to do it and then I just... went and did it. I'm glad I did, but it was predictable."

"What's wrong with predictable?" Faiz said. "Why do you two always want something else?"

"It doesn't make for a good story," Sairah smiled.

Chapter 13

Ghosts make sense. It doesn't feel like you can wipe out a whole person in an instant, erase them from existence. Lives end suddenly, abruptly, but personalities, memories, relationships, connections, the ways one person can alter others, don't work like that. You'd almost expect people to come back as ghosts. And they kind of do, in a way. One person can have even the slightest amount of influence on someone hundreds of years after their death.

Death feels so final, but it's more of a gaping absence than a dramatic end.

★ ★ ★

Preface to *Carolyn Hayward: A Local History Report* by Laana Hashmi:

> *The facts in this report are as accurate as possible. Most of the details of Carolyn Hayward's life are in dispute. I used facts which were corroborated by the highest number of sources I could find and indicated those sources where possible. But ultimately, it doesn't matter if she was born in 1852 or 1857 or when she graduated nursing school. The things that do matter, the accomplishments of her life, her work at the hospital and her dedication to children's healthcare have been backed up by the majority of sources.*

★ ★ ★

"Mom?" I said, carrying two crates down. "This is the last of them."

She came out of the kitchen to see the row of boxes. She looked around and wiped her hand across her forehead.

"I've gone through everything," I said. "The things I've decided to keep are in my room. The stuff I'm ready to give away is all here."

"But this is most of it," she said.

I shrugged. "I guess I don't need it."

"And the stuff you got from the library?"

"I returned it."

"Are you leaving soon then?"

"I think so. But I'll be back soon. I want to visit more."

She smiled. "That would be nice."

"It's not that far. I don't know why I made such a big deal of it." I turned to go back upstairs.

"You couldn't have known what was going to happen. And if you did, you would have done things differently."

I paused. "I know."

I didn't, yet.

★ ★ ★

From *Carolyn Hayward: A Local History Report* by Laana Hashmi, chapter titled "Childhood":

> As a child, Carolyn spent a lot of time in the hospital, often accompanying her parents on visits to oversee the building and its management. She befriended some of the doctors and nurses and learned basic skills, with many reports saying that before the age of ten she could dress a wound properly and by the time she was a teenager, she could even make splints.

★ ★ ★

"Hi. I'm Laana Hashmi. I sent you an email. I'm here to drop off a report," I said. "I just did some research and was wondering if you could add it to the website."

The receptionist nodded, her metallic City Hall name badge glinting under the fluorescent light. I pulled the report out of my tote bag and handed it to her over the counter.

"Carolyn Hayward?" she asked. "Creepy Carolyn?"

I laughed. "What were the stories you heard about her?"

"Just that she was a ghost. And she lived in that spooky house on Creep Hill."

"You never heard anything about how she died?"

"No," she shrugged. "Never really thought about it." She paused. "Her family did a lot of good, though. Wish I knew more about her."

★ ★ ★

From my report on Carolyn Hayward, chapter titled "Hobbies":

> *Not much is known about Carolyn's hobbies, but it's clear that she liked to read, and some sources say she painted the walls of the hospital's nursery. She also enjoyed gardening. Several sources state that Annabelle Hayward always took an interest in taking care of the plants and gardens in their compound and Carolyn continued to help maintain the grounds after her mother died.*

★ ★ ★

I hauled the plastic crate out of my car, filled with my own records and, on top, another printed copy of the research I had done on Carolyn.

"It's just like you said," I remarked as I set the crate on Taylor's desk in the back office of the record shop. "You live more than one life."

"I don't remember saying that," she said, leaning forward and picking up the report.

"I emailed you a copy too."

She leafed through the book. I saw her smile.

"Looks like you found a way to keep busy, apart from stacking CDs. And returning them, it looks like."

"Yeah, well, figured it was time to move on," I said. "Plus, it's all online now, and it's not like I can listen to these when they're here and I'm in the city."

"Are these all yours?" Taylor asked.

I nodded.

"What happened to your dad's records? Does he still have that huge collection?"

"Yeah. Still growing." Dad had given me the crate, filled with his records. I swapped them for my own right before leaving. Mine were just gathering dust. He needs the space more than I do.

"When are you leaving?"

"Soon."

"Like today?"

"Yeah, in a few hours."

"Okay, I'll go through these now to see how much I owe you."

"No, I don't want anything for them. But can you do me a favour?" I asked.

She nodded.

"Can you put this on your blog?" I gestured to the report. "I know it's not on topic, but I want people to know the truth."

"For sure."

"Thanks Taylor, for everything." As I turned to go, I saw a record Dad had mentioned but didn't have. There was no price sticker. "Hey Tay, how much for this?" I asked.

"It's all yours," she came out of the office.

"I can't —"

"Don't worry about it," she waved me away. "When are you coming back? Are we talking years again, or weeks or…"

"Months, hopefully."

"Great, then we don't have to say goodbye. You know how much I hate goodbyes."

"It's not a goodbye, I'll be back before you know it," I smiled.

"An 'I'll-see-you-in-a-bit.' Perfect," she grinned back, and hugged me anyway.

★ ★ ★

The thirteenth chapter in the report, "Death", was blank except for a single sentence:

Carolyn Hayward died of tuberculosis in 1889.

★ ★ ★

I handed Sairah the report. "I just dropped this off at City Hall, the library, school, and the hospital," I said. "And gave Taylor the report for her ghost blog. But I wanted you to see this section. I've bookmarked it for you."

Sairah opened the booklet where the bright orange sticky note was. "There was no fire at Hayward Manor during the time of Charles', Annabelle's or Carolyn Hayward's lives or deaths," she read out loud. "However, there was a fire on April the ninth, 2012." She looked up in disbelief.

"Keep going," I said.

"'That fire wasn't started by Sairah Awan, as previously believed, but by James Norcott, with assistance from Faiz Rizvi and Seth Hendricks'— wait, Seth was with them?"

"You remember him? I had to ask Faiz for his name."

"He helped?"

"Yeah, he wanted to make things right."

Sairah laughed. "Laana, when I said you could still do something about it, I meant you could just be more sensitive, not this." She looked up. "Thanks."

"You shouldn't have gone through that. And I should have done something about it a long time ago."

"Now people will know the truth."

"Yeah, we just have to hope they bother to read up to this part."

She flicked through the booklet. "You worked really hard on this. It's all very well-researched, I'm sure of it. As for being well-written —"

"Yeah, I should have asked for your help in that department," I admitted.

"You don't always have to do things on your own," Sairah said. "But you did good. You found out the truth about Carolyn and her life, not just the way she died."

★ ★ ★

Chapter titled "Legacy":

> Her goal was to improve the hospital's capacity to take care of children, which is why she created a specific wing for kids. The hospital's emphasis on the care of children was so strong that after her death, it became solely a children's hospital.
>
> Carolyn Hayward inspired a lot of ghost stories, almost all of them entirely fictional. Her true achievements and contributions were forgotten.

I never figured out what turned people into ghosts. If it was vengeance, it was only because we remembered her in the wrong way. We barely remembered the real Carolyn at all.

★ ★ ★

"I'll see you guys in October," I said, loading my suitcases into Dad's car. Mom and Dad were locking up the house. Sairah and Faiz stood in front of me.

"What am I supposed to do with my time now that I don't have some ghost to chase after?" Faiz grinned.

"Put that cinema pass to good use," I said.

"Same thing," he said.

Sairah gave me another hug, the third in the last twenty minutes "I know you," she said. "If you don't come that Saturday I am driving down and bringing you back myself. There's no stopping me!"

"I don't doubt it," I laughed. "I know you too."

Acknowledgements

An important part of this story is that we owe a lot to those who came before us. Thank you to my grandparents, my parents, my sister Zeina (who came after me but still), and to my uncles and aunts Tariq Samad, Karen Nemchik, and especially Neelofar and Hashmat Malik, who I was staying with when I started writing this book.

A huge, huge, thank you, of course, to Rebecca Wojturska and Haunt Publishing for believing in this story. To Kirstyn Smith for copyedits, Ross Stewart for proofreading, and Laura Jones-Rivera for typesetting. To Caroline Devereaux for the cover art, and Sun Hashmi for recommending Caroline. To Lauren T. Davila, who edited the anthology, *When Other People Saw Us, They Saw the Dead*, in which the short story version of this novel first appeared.

I am immensely grateful to my university professors/mentors Taije Silverman and Yolanda Wisher. And extra thank yous to Beth Kephart, who provided me advice on getting this book published, and Christine Woody, who taught me everything I know about Gothic literature.

To every editor in my work as a journalist who ever took a chance on me and my ideas and to those who continue to commission and edit me, thank you. You are all still helping me become a better writer.

To Allegra Frank and Ramya Pinninti for being there in spirit (and over text) throughout this whole process. To Maya Arthur who looked over my query letters and was an invaluable source of information about the publishing industry. To

Amy Song, who I vividly remember saying something along the lines of, "And if you're too smart they burn you for being a witch!" despite her having no recollection of this. She still very graciously gave me permission to use that line in this book and since this is the version of events I believe, I'll give credit where I think it's due.

And thank you to you, for reading this book!

The Credits

Creating a book takes a massive team effort. Haunt and Aliya Chaudhry would like to thank everyone who worked behind the scenes on *Every Version Ends in Death*.

Managing Director and Editor
Rebecca Wojturska

Copy-editor
Kirstyn Smith

Proofreader
Ross Stewart

Designer
Caroline Devereaux

Typesetter
Laura Jones-Rivera

About the Author

Aliya Chaudhry is a fiction writer and journalist. As a journalist, she has covered music and internet culture for publications including Alternative Press, The Daily Beast, Kerrang!, MTV, NME, Slate, Stereogum, The Verge and VICE. She has lived in the United Kingdom, Pakistan, the United States and Kenya and is currently based in London. Her short story "The Ghost of Creek Hill", an extract of what became *Every Version Ends in Death*, was previously published in Haunt Publishing's May 2022 anthology *When Other People Saw Us, They Saw The Dead*. This is her first novel.